UNTAMED: HOUSE OF BERSERKERS

Wicked Reform School

LACEY CARTER ANDERSEN

Copyright 2020
Published by Lacey Carter Andersen
Cover art and design by Silviya Yordanova of DARK IMAGINARIUM Art
Editing by Michelle Lobo
Formatted By: Kassie Morse

This work of fiction is intended for mature audiences only. All characters are over the age of eighteen. Names, characters, places, and incidents are either a product of the author's imagination or are used fictitiously. Any resemblance to any persons, living or dead, business establishments, events, or locales is entirely coincidental.

This book is protected under the copyright laws of the United States of America. Any reproduction or other unauthorized use of the material or artwork herein is prohibited without the express written permission of the author.

To my kids-- Staying inside together has had its challenges, but thank you for giving your mama time to write.

~ Lacey Carter Andersen

Chapter One

KIERA

The music pounds all around me and every drunken twenty-something year old in our berserker community drinks from red plastic cups as they shout along to the song. Outside the windows of the house, bonfires burn in every direction, lighting the night in a fiery orange glow, and the heavy scent of burning wood and smoke fills the air.

The fires were a reminder to us all that this wasn't just a celebration. It was a night when the line between us and the spirit world was thin…thinner than any other day of the year.

A night where *anything* could happen.

I grin as I push my way through everyone. But each time someone spots me they drunkenly scream, "Happy graduation!" Or "Happy Walpurgisnacht!"

I thank everyone I pass, smiling so much my face hurts. In the eyes of our community, I wouldn't be seen as an adult for another ten or more years, but this was the closest that I've gotten. I'd passed out of our tiny community college, and soon I'd be assigned a position.

No more classes. No more grades.

I was ecstatic!

And what was more, this day was special. Starting today, all berserkers would celebrate Walpurgisnacht for the next two weeks. It would be a time of drinking, laughter, and relaxing. A time when graduates got a break before real life began. A time when the adults in our community got to relax and just be people.

It was my favorite celebration of the year, despite the strange prickling of magic that always seemed to fill the air. Despite the fact that it was the only time when the branding on my arm tingled at midnight, awakening me from my sleep. Ignoring the feeling was a small price to pay for Walpurgisnacht. Every berserker simply knew that this was a time of fun, and only dangerous if you were dumb enough to engage the spirt world.

Shoving my way through the massive guys, I roll my eyes. Over the years, I'd *mostly* gotten used to the fact that I was one of the only petite berserkers in our community. Even compared to the women, I was small. But when I had to make my way through crowds of guys, it was almost impossible. Every fucking berserker male was built like a bus, even when they weren't in their other form, which made it hard for me to get anywhere.

Unless of course I went a little crazy and started punching them in the dicks.

I think about it for a second, then sigh. It was a happy day. I shouldn't ruin it by going on a dick punching rampage. That always put the fellas in a bad mood.

One berserker draws my gaze by itching around the outside of the blood-red symbol burned into his arm, a symbol that every one of us had. *Busted*.

"Charlie…"

His gaze jerks up, and I see it in his eyes. He knows he's

been caught. As the daughter of the Lord of the Winter Berserkers, I usually *tried* to uphold the rules of the community. At least with the younger, more vulnerable members of our house.

"Should you really be here?" I ask, lifting a brow.

He blushes and draws his hand back from his new branding, running his fingers through his dark hair. "I'm not drinking. Honest."

Berserkers got their brands at sixteen, so Charlie was way too young to be at a party with all of the graduates, and those that had long since been branded. And yet, our people were different than most. A family. And we looked out for everyone, old or young.

"Just get home before things get too crazy."

He smiles. "Will do."

The music suddenly cuts off, and I push past more massive men to spot Charlie's older brother on the small stage in the living room. He lifts a beer to the crowd. "Tonight we drink in celebration!"

Everyone cheers and lifts their own drinks.

"We, the children of the Vikings, we, children of the bear, we drink because we live!"

More cheers.

And then his gaze searches out his brother in the crowd. "Tonight, my brother became one of us. He now wears the brand of a berserker, the axe. It will remind him of our heritage. It will remind him that a berserker can never be stopped. That we can cut through anything and everything to reach what we need." Then his gaze ran over the crowd. "It stands for the strength and bravery that must burn within all berserkers, but especially the Winter Berserkers. Long live the House of Winter!"

This time, even I cheer. Charlie's brother could be a drunken fool, but his words awakened within me the pride

I felt the night I was branded. The pride all of us felt. My hand strokes the marking on my arm…two diamonds on top of each other, and the line that slides through the center of both. Beneath my touch, I felt it. The magic that always hummed just below the surface.

And then the music was turned on once more, and the spell was broken. We were no longer the proud children of the Viking berserkers. We were just a bunch of crazy youth celebrating all the accomplishments of the year.

Continuing through the living room, I search for my best friends but find them nowhere, so I switch directions. When I reach the kitchen, I finally spot my closest group of troublemaking buddies pulled off to one corner, talking in low voices. *Oh, this should be good.* I sprint over to them.

"What are we plotting?"

They look up, and Keith and Payton grin when they see it's me. Most brothers in our community looked similar, but Keith and Payton could've passed for twins, with their heads of shaggy brown hair, big brown eyes, and disastrous taste in clothes.

"We want to have a good time," Keith whispers.

Lucy, a stunning woman with a huge mass of dark, curly hair, and the most flawless dark skin, leans down and whispers in my ear, "We're going to hit a human club."

My lips spread into a smile. It wasn't that we weren't allowed to go to the human town not far from our small community, it was simply *strongly* suggested that we stay away. The adults came and went as they pleased, but with the young men's abilities still so strongly tied to their emotions, our age group mostly stayed here.

"I think," I begin slowly, and they all watch me, "that sounds like an awesome idea!"

Lucy squeals, and then we're laughing and racing out the backdoor.

Even though females don't "go berserk," we tend to be faster and more agile than our male counterparts. So while Keith and Payton start out leading us to their dad's truck, Lucy and I quickly overtake them as we race through the woods. I hear the boys shout their protests, but we just keep going, grinning ear-to-ear.

Beneath the shadows of the woods, I feel the spirits. They race along beside us, howling their eerie songs, their dark hands reaching for us out of the protection of the fire light.

But we are berserkers…we're *untouchable*.

And so even though they howl, even though the forest is alive with them, we're not afraid. The branding on my arm burns when they draw too close, but I push down the pain. Let them come for us! Even without my axes, I have the blood of my Viking ancestors running through my veins.

I roar as a spirit blocks our path and dive through the shadowy being. Lucy roars beside me, and we keep going, without hesitation. Like the bear, we fear nothing.

Exploding out of the woods, we spot the boys' cabin. Tonight, all the adults celebrate in the great hall. And the elderly watch the young together. The rest of our town…it belongs to us. So, we don't bother hiding, we just circle toward our escape vehicle.

When the boys arrive, Lucy and I are stretched across the hood of their truck, trying to look like we hadn't just barely beaten them. Our breath still comes out fast and our hearts pound.

"What took you so long?" I ask.

Payton rolls his eyes. "Just get in the car."

Lucy and I climb into the bed of the truck, and I knock the top of the roof, telling the boys to get going shortly after they slam the door. Payton starts the engine, and then we're squealing out into the night, taking the back roads out of town, our enthusiasm palpable.

I lean over the side of the truck, letting my long white-blonde hair fly wildly around me. Part of me wishes that I'd chosen a different outfit for a night spent with the humans. Our people tended to stick to wearing a lot of leather and fur, being natural-born hunters and all, so my current outfit wasn't exactly nightclub trendy. I wore brown leather pants that were so well-worn that they were soft as butter against my skin. My top was my favorite style, a leather vest, backless, strung together by leather cords of string.

My dad hated this outfit. My brothers threatened to burn it.

I smile into the wind. *So maybe it wasn't human club appropriate, but hopefully that meant it was sexy.*

"Did you see that?"

I turn to face Lucy. She's staring out at the woods, concern on her face.

My gaze moves to the trees that whip by. "I don't see anything."

She runs a hand nervously through those amazing dark curls of hers. "I thought I saw a bear."

I stiffen. Seeing a bear was usually a good sign. But on Walpurgisnacht, it was sometimes a warning. A warning of death to come.

"Do you want to go back?"

The air seems to fly around us, and my best friend's gaze meets mine. For a second the world fades away around us, and it's just us. Whatever she decides now, I'll do. Berserkers trust their gut, and I trust Lucy's instincts as much as I trust my own.

And then she smiles. "It was probably nothing. Just a shadow."

"You sure?"

She laughs. "The spirits always love to mess with us."

I smile and lean back against the side of the truck, feeling the tension in my body ease. She was right. The damned spirits would try to ruin our night of fun.

She kicks the bottom of my foot. "Did you talk to your dad about spending a couple weeks traveling before real life begins?"

I sigh and let my head fall back, drinking in the light of the full moon above us and the sea of stars. My father was Lord of the Winter Berserkers. He expected me to help lead the people of our town. He expected me to represent our family well at all times. When I spoke about leaving, even for a little while, his knee-jerk reaction was to say no. I had long ago accepted that he was worried I wouldn't come back. He didn't understand that I wanted to see the world, but that the Winter Woods would always be my home.

"Earth to Kiera!"

I laugh and look back at her. "Not yet, but I will."

"Promise?"

"Promise."

She claps her hands together, her dimples appearing. In that moment, she reminds me of when she was a little girl. Before she threw out her dresses and started spinning her swords. "We're going to see the ocean! And surfers! We're going to climb mountain tops, and fuck hot boys."

I laugh. "And more."

"And more," she repeats.

And, I swear, this night can't get any better. It's... perfect. The end of one chapter in our lives and the beginning of so much more.

It takes us about thirty minutes to reach the human town. Winter Bend isn't exactly a big city, but there were two clubs and three bars open late at night, and the humans tended to drink enough not to ask too many questions about the strange people that came down every so often from the Winter Woods, all with a matching symbol burned into their arms.

Not that they know the symbol is an ancient one, burned into every berserker at the age of sixteen. When people ask about it, we just distract them from the topic. Even though they probably thought it meant we were some kind of fucking cult.

After driving along the outside of our favorite club, we find it packed and have to circle around and park in the back. I leap from the car in one smooth motion, giddy with excitement, before Lucy climbs down and kicks my shoe lightly.

"Humans don't leap from cars like the hulk," she scolds me.

I lean closer. "Humans don't talk about humans like they aren't humans either," I joke.

She smirks, and the boys climb out of the car and look at us.

Keith wiggles his brows. "What should we do first?"

"Dance!" I shout, then amend my answer. "Drink a ton, then dance."

He grins like a fool and holds out his arm. "My lady."

"Good sir," I say, tilting my imaginary hat to him and taking his arm.

And just like that, the four of us saunter up to the club like we have a dozen times before. The bouncer takes one look at Lucy and I, then gestures for us to go right on in. I toss my white-blonde hair over my shoulder, trying to look all hot and badass, and then we walk, our super cool walk, right on inside.

Two guys send drinks my way before I even get the

chance to order. I share them with my friends, then grab the shots we ordered and down those too. By the time we do a second shot, we're all pretty damned wasted. You'd think with how much we ate, and how great our metabolisms were, that we'd handle alcohol well.

It's the opposite though. We're freaking light weights.

Suddenly some asshole crashes into Keith, then hits on me. Keith's smile fades and he gives the guy his "don't mess with me" look. Every single berserker knows better than to push us when we are mad. We were taught from an early age about meditating, breathing deeply, and walking away. But the human pokes his finger at Keith, and there's one god damn second when the music melts away, and I swear Keith's muscles start to swell.

And then Lucy presses herself against him, and his size seems to deflate in an instant.

"Come on," I tell them. "Let's get some air on the balcony."

We hurry outside, and for the millionth time in my life I try not to be annoyed that the guys around us seem to go berserk at the drop of a hat. Yeah, maybe I'm not very sympathetic, but having five older brothers means that I am forever reminding them to go meditate, practice their breathing, or take a break.

And sometimes a girl just wants to have fun.

As we push through the crowd to reach the balcony outside, a man slams into me, and I have to turn to avoid the half a dozen tall men that follow after him. Some instinct in the back of my mind, a weird prickling of the hairs at my neck, makes me pause and watch them as they start to blend into the crowd. There was something about the men…something not human.

Yeah, we have vampires, shifters, demons, and even the occasional fae that make their way through this town, a pit stop before they get to a big city, but something about those men set me on edge. There was just something off about them.

And the more I stared after them, the more I was sure of it…they weren't human.

"Kiera?"

I look back at Keith. "Did you see those guys?"

He frowns. "There's a lot of guys."

Turning around, I see that the strange group of men is gone from view. And yet, the lingering feeling that something's wrong remains. *It's probably just Walpurgisnacht and the damn spirits*, I tell myself.

"You coming?" I hear Lucy say behind me.

I shake off the weird feeling and go to enjoy life with my friends. They salute my graduation. Lucy grumbles about how she has another year of schooling, and the boys cheers themselves for finishing last year and still managing to maintain their social lives.

All and all, we sit at our table, with the night's temperature perfect beyond words, and the scents of the city and the forest around us. I smile so much my face hurts, and when Lucy heads for the bathroom, I lean in conspiratorially with the guys and finally ask Keith if he has a thing for her.

His cheeks turn red. "She's just a friend."

I smirk. "None of her other friends are constantly checking out her ass."

His blush deepens. "I don't. But, I mean, do you think I'd ever have a shot with her?"

I take a long drawl of my beer. I wasn't going to reveal what Lucy had told me, but both men had a good chance of becoming her next boyfriends. "It doesn't hurt to try."

"It hurt when we tried to ask you out," Payton mutters.

I freeze. "We were like eight."

"Yeah, but Emory had such a thing for you that when he found out he kicked our asses."

Keith laughs, crinkles forming at the corners of his eyes. "Just be glad he hadn't hit puberty. Can you imagine that beating in his berserker form?"

The two go off about the fight, but suddenly the night seems a little less fun. Every time I think of Emory, it's like a face full of cold water. He'd been my best friend. We'd decided, as innocent, young children, that we'd get married someday. We were too young to really know what that meant, but the connection between us had been real. Deep.

And then, he'd just disappeared.

"He had it so bad for you," Keith suddenly tells me, breaking into my thoughts.

I wince. "Nah, if he liked me that much, he would've taken the time to say goodbye when he left."

"Yeah, that was kind of weird," Payton says softly, and I think the assholes finally just remembered that I don't like it when they talk about him.

There's an awkward silence for half a second before Keith suddenly straightens. "Has Lucy been gone for a while?"

I frown. I wouldn't say she'd been gone that long. But when I think back to the strange group of men, I find myself standing. "I'll go look for her."

"Want us to come with you?" Keith asks, starting to rise.

I shake my head. "I think you two in the women's room might be a problem."

He grins and salutes me with his drink.

"I'll be fast," I say. "She probably just got distracted by some hottie."

"Better not have," I hear Keith mumble under his breath.

I would've laughed if I wasn't feeling so on edge. It kind of bugs me that I'd been so troubled by some strange men that I might actually be letting them ruin my night. So I promise myself the second I see Lucy safe and sound, I'd push them out of my thoughts.

Making my way through the club, I shoot down four men and shove aside a fifth as I wind my way to the bathrooms in the back. All along, my gaze sweeps the club for any sign of Lucy safely flirting with a sexy human, and in the back of my mind, any sign of the men.

But when I don't see her or them, I start to worry more.

Rushing to the bathroom, I push past the line of angry women as they shout after me and then search all the stalls, despite the protests of a few surprised women. When I realize she isn't here, I go back out into the hall, feeling nervous. She wasn't in the club, on the dance floor, on the balcony, or in the bathroom. *Where could she be?*

Looking down to the end of the hall, my heart thuds as I stare at the two security guards flanking both sides of a door that says "VIP." There's no way in hell Lucy would just take off to the room, not without at least shooting us a text if some rich asshole had invited her in. But it was either the VIP room or outside, and I knew she wouldn't have just left.

Making my way to the door, the two security guys stiffen at my approach.

"Only VIPs allowed," one of them barks.

I lift a brow. "I'm just looking for a friend. She's, as she'd put it, a dark goddess with the kind of hair any woman would die for. You seen her?"

"No," he says, but I don't like how quickly he responds.

Oh hell, the hairs on the back of my neck are standing on end again.

"Well, maybe I'll just take a look to be sure." I take a step closer.

The big guy moves to block my path. "Only VIPs allowed."

I flash him a smile that's all teeth. Both of them are easily double my size, but they're only human. "Get out of my way and this doesn't have to hurt."

He leans down so that his hot breath is on my face. "Back away."

I'm debating about the wisdom of beating up a couple of humans when I hear Lucy scream beyond the door. My vision goes black, and I move without thinking, slamming my fist into one guard's face, then spinning to kick the other one in the junk.

When the guy grabs his nose, blood spurting out between his fingertips, I sweep his legs out from under him and watch as he hits the ground, hard. Not hesitating a second longer, I kick open the door and race inside.

And there in the back of a darkened room I see my Lucy bound and bleeding, her face a swollen mess, and the strange men from earlier surrounding her. They turn, flashing their fangs, and something inside of me goes cold.

There's no damned way that I can fight seven vampires and survive, but I sure as hell am going to die trying.

Chapter Two

KIERA

*L*ucy says something around the gag in her mouth, and a vampire turns and punches her in the face, knocking her back so hard on the ground that she lays there, unmoving. My heart stops as I stare at her, and I'm shocked when I realize she isn't breathing.

No, this isn't possible.

But no matter how long I stare, her chest doesn't rise and fall.

Something terrible awakens inside of me. Something born of anger and rage.

The vampires rush toward me, and I fully expect them to attack. I expect them to use their incredible strength against my small body, and break me piece by piece.

But when they get closer, they skid to a stop.

My view of them turns red and hazy. My thoughts race away. I realize that I'm swelling, growing, changing, but it's like my brain doesn't care. All it sees is them.

And what it wants to do.

When the first two attack, I'm not thinking or planning. Usually fighting against bigger opponents requires strategy, but it's like my brain doesn't work. Instead, my body seems to react without thought. And to my shock, it works in a way I never imagined.

My hand reaches out and snaps the neck of a vampire, tossing him aside like a rag doll.

A roar fills my head, a roar I realize might be coming from me, and I grab two vampires and slam them together, over and over again until they collapse, unmoving. I continue toward the three remaining vampires that stand between me and Lucy, my steps seem too slow, and the ground seems to shake beneath my feet.

"Stop," one of the vampires says. "Do you know who I am?"

One of them rushes at me. I grab his arms as he tries to attack and pull until his eyes go wide and blood gurgles out of his mouth, his body stretching past its limit. When he stops breathing, I let him drop to the ground. My gaze snaps to the other one that had approached. He tries to run around me, to escape, but I wrap my hands around his head and crush his skull in.

When the final vampire cowers back from me, I stomp toward him.

"I am a vampire prince, a pure breed, a leader of my people. If you kill me, there will be no place you can go. There will be—"

I punch him in the face. He smashes back onto the ground, and I leap on top of him. My fists pummel him, and I see nothing through the red of my anger. Nothing at all. But I feel the blood as it coats my fists. I hear the sounds of him screaming, and then a terrible gurgling, and then nothing.

Finally, I stop. I'm breathing hard. Overwhelmed by emotion.

My gaze moves and lands on Lucy where she lies still

on the ground. I move away from the dead vampire and kneel down beside her. I touch her throat, searching for a pulse, and find none. I shake her gently. I listen for a heartbeat.

There's nothing.

My rage fades away, replaced by a horrifying sadness.

I feel my body shrink. I feel my muscles grow smaller, and then the haze of red fades away, and it's only me. Kneeling before a girl I grew up with. A woman I played with as a baby, walked with as a toddler, and enjoyed life with as an adult.

And the vampires had killed her...for what?

Tears rain down my cheeks, splattering on her still body. None of this made any sense. Why would vampires come here just to beat the shit out of one of our people? They were assholes, but this was just violence, for no reason.

Something subtle changes in the air. I turn and realize that red sparks are drifting into the air from my berserker branding. Something I've never seen before. Something I've never heard of before. They float about the room like glowing embers, then settle on Lucy. Her skin is illuminated for a moment, like a nephilim, and then the sparks fade into nothing.

I watch my best friend through my tears, hoping, praying that the magic in the air this night might save her. But whatever that was, it didn't matter. Lucy was still dead.

I'm so overcome by grief that I don't realize that someone has entered the room until I hear a curse spoken from the doorway. My head jerks around, and I stiffen, staring at a massive man.

His hair is dark brown, his matching beard wild and untamed, and his eyes are the same blue as the purest waters. He wears a grey t-shirt that strains across his muscled chest, arms swirling with black tattoos are clenched at his sides. Almost hidden amongst the tattoos is his berserker branding, and on his back he carries a sword.

At his side, both the guards stand, glaring at me. The massive man draws a sword from his back, and to my shock, cuts the heads off both the men beside him. Then he slams the door closed. Stalking toward me, he cuts the head off every vampire on his way to me like a professional executioner.

Holy hell. I reach for my axes, then remember they're still lying on my bed at home. *Fuck.*

"What do you want?" I say, intending to sound threatening, and instead sounding lost.

"You…you went berserk," he responds, his voice barely louder than a whisper.

"No." I shake my head. "I'm a woman…I can't…that's not—"

"You went berserk, and the guards told people. More people than me." This time his words sound tense, almost frightened.

I shake my head again. *No, I didn't.* I don't know what I did, but women don't go berserk. At least, there are only a few stories about female berserkers, and there's no way I'm one of them.

I was just trying to help Lucy.

"Kiera, we have to go. Now!"

"What? No." I look from Lucy then back to him. "How did you know my name?"

"It doesn't matter," he rushes out, then reaches his hand out to me. "If we don't leave now, you're going to be in more trouble than you can imagine. These vampires are important. If they find out what you did, you're dead."

His words send ice through my blood. I reach for his hand and let him pull me to my feet. Suddenly, he's just a massive man, towering over me, his frame almost surrounding me. A tremble moves through me, and I look back at Lucy's still body.

Suddenly, he begins to tug me to a back door.

"But I don't understand—"

"We'll talk later," he rushes out, resheathing his sword. "Right now we need to run."

I hear something crash behind us. Turning, I spot a group of men in suits in the open doorway. They look between the room full of dead people and us, their eyes wide.

The big man scoops me into his arms and starts to run for the back door.

"Stop!" someone shouts, but he only speeds up.

I flinch at the sound of a gun going off, and the steps of the man who holds me falter before he's running once more. We explode out the door and into the night. He holds me close as we run for the end of the alley, but just as I think we might make it, more men in suits step in front of us.

He doesn't miss a beat, spinning on his heel and running back the way we came.

But the men that were inside pile out, blocking our view.

All of them have guns pointed at him.

His grip tightens around me, and I swear he's going to charge through them, but then one man shouts, "Aim for the girl!" And all their guns point at me.

It's strange how fast he stops then. Almost instantly. So fast that I look up into his face, trying to figure out what just happened.

His crystal blues eyes look down on me. "Tell them I did it. Do you understand?"

"Like hell." I didn't care what he said. I attacked the

vampires, and they damned well deserved it. I wasn't going to let this mysterious stranger take the fall for me.

"Don't be a fool," he hisses. "Do as I—"

The men surround us. I'm wrenched from his grip, and a growl tears from his lips.

They remove his sword from his back and handcuff him roughly. His face is a mask of tension, but he doesn't fight back.

"No!" finally drops from my lips, but everyone ignores me as they wrestle him to the ground. "No," I say, louder this time. "It wasn't him. It was me!"

The man behind me chuckles. "There's no way you killed those men."

"I did!"

"A group of pure breed fucking vampires," he huffs. "I don't think so."

"I did," I say again. "I—I went berserk."

The alley goes silent. Then the stranger who rescues me swears. "She didn't go berserk. She's my fucking lover, and she's fucking trying to protect me."

"I'm not!" I tell them. "I killed them! They tortured Lucy! They killed her—" Tears choke my throat. "They deserved what they got."

"What do we do?" one of the men asks.

The man behind me sighs and jerks my hands, suddenly slamming handcuffs around them. "Take them both. We'll get to the bottom of this."

For the first time, the strange man starts to fight them. But within seconds, a needle is shoved into his neck, and he goes limp. Already I can see the four gunshot wounds in his back, and the pools of blood growing beneath his shirt. *What more had they done to him?* Bile rises in the back of my throat. *Is he okay?*

We're dragged to a black van that waits for us at the

end of the alley. The men in suits are all around us, creating a circle as if to hide us from the sight of the humans.

When I look up at the end of the alley, I see Keith and Payton staring down at us from the balcony, mouths gaping open.

"The vampires killed Lucy!" I shout at them. "So I went berserk and killed them all!"

Keith's face goes white.

Payton shakes his head as if nothing I say can be true.

I open my mouth to say more, but I'm tossed into the back of the van alongside the strange man, and the doors close. My heart pounds wildly. Yeah, I knew I should never talk about going berserk in front of humans, but I needed to tell them. They needed to know so they could tell my family.

Because I was pretty sure wherever I was going, I might not see them again.

It was probably my imagination, but I swear I hear the spirits laughing at us in the darkness.

Chapter Three

KIERA

In the back of the van I instinctually move closer to the strange man and away from the guards who sit by the door. My hands are cuffed behind my back, but I surprise myself by lying against him. I had no idea who he was. I had no idea why he'd tried to help me. But in this van, he was my only ally.

Tears roll down my cheeks as I think of Lucy, and the events of that room roll through my mind. Female berserkers weren't nearly as strong as their male counterparts, but one punch shouldn't have killed her.

But then, if that vampire had been an alpha vampire, a first of his kind, that would explain why he was so powerful. And if he was a vampire prince, in all likelihood he could've been an alpha. So maybe that explained why he was so strong, but it *didn't* explain why I was able to kill him so easily.

I think of the haze of red, of my slow steps and my powerful movements. Yes, I'd publicly declared that I'd gone berserk, but some part of me had never believed it. I was twenty-three. Most berserker males lost control as soon as they hit puberty. If I had the ability, wouldn't it have awakened sooner than now?

And what did I know about female berserkers with the ability? Only that they were more legend than reality. And something about a prophecy that I can't seem to remember.

I press my face against the strange man's chest and breathe in his scent. It's surprisingly…pleasant, almost comforting, like warm caramel and vanilla. Some unexpected awareness inside of me realizes that it's his natural scent, and it makes something inside of me tighten. I look up into his face, the lights from the street lamps illuminating us where we lay every so often.

In slumber, his face is peaceful. Nice. *More* than nice. He's easily the most handsome man I've ever seen. His cheekbones are high for a man's, and his lashes are long and dark. His beard is wild, but there's something interesting about it, like it hides the face of a remarkably beautiful man. Everything about him seems normal, and yet he's lying beside me bleeding from bullet wounds he took to protect me.

It made no sense.

They killed Lucy, so I killed them. That was all I understood.

More tears roll down my cheeks and fill my eyes. I don't understand what I'm doing when I press my face to his neck. I just…I feel so lost. So afraid.

"Kiera?" My name comes out groggy.

I stiffen and pull back from the man. His eyes are open, and he stares down at me as if he thinks I might be a dream.

"How do you know my name?"

His eyes close again, and I swear I can hear his heart

racing. *Is he refusing to tell me? Or is the medicine or the pain keeping him from explaining himself clearly?*

"What are you?" I ask instead.

He answers, his face twisted in pain. "A berserker."

"The bullets—"

"I'll be fine," he says.

One of the men in suits kicks at my leg. "Quiet, you two!"

The stranger leans closer until his hot breath tickles my ear. "Don't tell them what you did. Let me take the fall. Trust me. It's the only way to keep you safe."

But why is it so important to you to keep me safe?

Our van rolls to a stop. A minute later, the doors to the back of the van are pulled open and they reach inside and grab us, yanking us out.

The strange man growls again, a warning in the back of his throat. But when I look at him, he's not glaring at the men who handle him so roughly, he's looking at the men touching me.

My breath catches in my throat. Berserkers can be protective, it's their nature, but I don't think any man has ever looked at me like that before.

We're hauled up the steps of a random brown building and pulled inside to a hall illuminated by fluorescent light that slowly opens up into a large room. Men in suits work at desks crammed together in the space, but all eyes go to us as they drag us through the room and down a quiet hallway.

When they stop before a door and shove me inside, the strange man begins to shout in the hall before the door closes behind me. They plunk me onto one of two chairs that face each other, a table between them, before uncuffing my hands and then chaining them to the table.

I look up to see a mirror in front of me, and I've seen

enough cop shows to be pretty sure there are men on the other side watching me. For the first time since killing the vampires, the reality of my situation really dawns on me. Everything the strange man said sinks into my consciousness, and I realize that I really am in deep shit.

If I killed a group of vampires, if I killed an alpha vampire, I'd have to hope like hell they wouldn't treat me as an adult in the eyes of the court. At twenty-three, the paranormal world still considered me an adolescent. It wasn't until we hit thirty that we were tried for crimes as adults, but they made exceptions.

And I'm pretty sure killing a room full of men would be an exception.

Most adults tried for murder were executed within days of sentencing. When the stranger warned me about not speaking, he'd been right. Yet I couldn't stomach the idea of letting him take the fall for me. *Was he an adult? Would they kill him for my crime?*

As I'm mulling over what the hell to do, the door to my little room opens. A man stands in the doorway, a young man with neat black hair, dark brown eyes, and a crisp, expensive-looking suit. He plays with his cufflinks for a moment as he stares at me, then flashes a smile before turning and closing the door behind him.

When he looks back, that smile of his widens. "I have a feeling we're going to end up doing this the hard way, and I fucking love the hard way."

My stomach sinks. *What the hell does that mean?*

Chapter Four

EMORY

I'm slumped into a chair, my hands chained to the table before I can summon the strength to fight to reach Kiera. The bullets in my back burn and the blood that leaks from the wounds are hot on my back, but unfortunately for these Enforcers, I'm well equipped to handle pain.

The shot they gave me would've put another man out for hours, but I was experienced with it. I'd been given it hundreds of times in the past, and developed more of a resistance to it than most. And yet, it had still been enough to keep me from changing, to keep me from going berserk and killing the Enforcers who took Kiera from me.

Just the thought of her makes my stomach twist.

I'd been sent specifically to monitor Drake and his vampire posse. There were whispers that the vampire was being hunted, and so I'd been dispatched by the king to help the alpha vampire in his time of need. The assignment had made me sick. The bastard was twisted and rotten to the core. He liked to kill for pleasure. He liked to take young women to dominate and frighten.

The vampires that guarded him never blinked an eye at what he did, but it tortured me. I couldn't bear to see women hurt. I couldn't bear to see the pointless violence. And yet, that's exactly why my brother had sent me on this mission…to torture me, to break me even more.

When my assignment had led us to this town, I'd thought it was the final nail in my coffin. A reminder of just how far I'd fallen. As a child, this area had been my home. It had been the place where every good memory I'd ever had had taken place, so it seemed like a cruel injustice that I'd be brought back to this place of innocence, when I was nothing but a shell of a man.

I'd sat at the bar, remembering this place. Remembering my best friend Kiera, and wishing more than anything that my mother hadn't taken everything from me. And then, then I'd flipped on the security camera on my cellphone, praying they were done with whoever they were hurting that night.

The last thing I'd expected was to see Kiera Frost.

That white-blonde hair of hers, streaming down past her thighs, was unlike any other woman's. That, combined with being in this town, and seeing the familiar leather clothes of the Winter Berserkers, and I knew it could only be her.

And yet, as she stood by the door, her face pale, I recognized that she was no longer a girl; she was a woman. An impossibly beautiful woman.

And then she'd gone berserk.

And everything changed.

The door to the room I'm being kept in opens, and a woman enters. Her eyes are cold and her jet black hair is short and neat. She wears a dark blue suit, tailored to fit her petite frame.

I expect others to join her, but she closes the door

behind her, leaving the tiny woman alone in a room with a potentially dangerous berserker. My gaze snaps to the window that I'm sure others watch me through, but even I realize that if I wanted to kill the woman, the help on the side of the window would be too late.

"I'm Agent Jami," she says, her voice as cold as her eyes.

I stare back at her, not blinking.

"And you are?"

Again, I don't answer.

Her mouth lifts into a chilling smile. "I know exactly who you are, Emory. What I don't understand is what the hell you're doing. There's a woman just next door who has taken responsibility for the death of the—"

"I did it, not her."

She moves closer to me and stands in front of the table, setting her hands down on top of it. "If she actually went berserk, you and I both know how valuable she is."

"She didn't. She's lying to cover for me."

Her calculating gaze runs over my face, but I'd withstood enough torture to keep my face carefully blank. "You can get up right now, and I'll return you to the custody of your brother."

And I knew exactly what would happen to Kiera. If they believed she went berserk, her fate would be worse than death. And if they just thought I was letting an innocent woman take the fall for my crime, they'd kill her fast and clean.

"It was me," I tell her, no hesitation in my voice.

They'll have to kill me for this, no matter how powerful my family is.

And death will be a relief.

"Just say she did it," she presses again, then leans

closer, lowering her voice. "Do you think I want to deal with the repercussions with your family for this?"

"I killed the vampires, all of them."

She curses.

A second later, the door opens and a man stands without speaking. A painfully thin man, so thin that he looks sickly fragile. His hair is slicked back, and his long nose seems to stand out from his wrinkled face. If not for the cruelty in his dark eyes, I might have felt pity for him.

Instead, I knew exactly who he was. And I knew the same thing the agent did: my time to escape was gone.

The head Enforcer was here.

Chapter Five

KIERA

I want to look away from the man as he sits down across from me, but I get the feeling it'd be the equivalent of taking my eyes off a spider, a creepy fucking spider with legs bent, ready to attack. And every berserker knew not to take their eyes off of an enemy.

"So." He fiddles with those damn cufflinks again. "You probably want to deny killing the vampires. You want to tell us that the other man killed them."

I lift a brow. "Not at all."

His cool exterior crumbles for a moment. "No?"

A shudder moves through my body. *I have to do this, no matter what happens.* "I killed them."

"You went berserk?" he asks, lifting a brow.

I nod.

Something changes in his expression that I don't understand. He rises from his chair and moves about the room, as if pacing. Suddenly, his hand slides the light switch off. I hear the scraping of a chair, and I start to stand, but the cuffs keep me bound to the table.

And then he's behind me, his hands wrapped around my throat, keeping me in place against him.

"Wh—?" His hands tighten, cutting off the word.

I hear people banging against the door, but something prevents it from opening.

"Listen to me," he growls into my ear. "Haven't you heard about the damned prophecy? The one that says a berserker female will be the wife to the one male capable of ruling over all the berserkers? No?" he scoffs. "You probably haven't. But I'll tell you this, if the House of Berserkers hears about your existence, you're going to wish for death. So tell them you killed those vamps, tell them you didn't, but don't tell them that you went berserk. You understand me?"

The pounding at the door grows louder.

"I don't understand," I force past my lips.

He pulls me back harder against him. "The leader of the House of Berserkers is a fucking beast. I'm a cold fucking shifter, but even I can't handle that monster. If you have a choice between death and the berserkers, choose death."

Suddenly, the door bursts open.

He's away from me in an instant. The light flashes on, revealing his chair on its side beside the door. Two giant men in suits stand in the doorway, both frowning.

"What the hell happened?"

The Enforcer shrugs, adjusting his cufflinks again. "A miscommunication." Then his eyes swing to me. "Confession time, girl…"

I draw myself up taller and speak before I know what I'm saying. "I killed them, but I didn't go berserk."

The Enforcer's expression gives nothing away.

Suddenly, all the men pull back. An old man that reeks

of death comes through the door, his piercing black eyes almost painful when they fall on me.

His thin lips pull back. "What say you?"

My heart races. "I killed the vampires."

My Enforcer bows his head slightly. "It's an issue, sir. Both of them claim to be the murderer, and until we can get to the bottom of who—"

"They will both go to the Wicked Reform School." His voice is a raspy declaration.

"But, sir," My Enforcer begins. "Those vampires were important. Their families will want the responsible party killed, so—"

The old man's gaze snaps to the Enforcer and within seconds the man is on his knees, gasping for breath. "I will not execute the wrong party. Nor will I execute a minor." His eyes snap back to me, and the Enforcer drops to the ground, finally drawing in full breaths. "If they cannot be reformed, then they shall die."

Someone in the hall says, "The House of Berserkers will want—"

"The House of Berserkers do *not* rule here, the *law* does!" Anger laces the old man's words, and then his gaze narrows on me. "Reform or die, berserker, that's your only choice."

When he leaves the room, my knees buckle and I fall back into my chair. T*he Wicked Reform School? No, I'd heard about that place.*

The Enforcer might have said my choices were death or life as a bride to a monster, but it seems there's always another horrible choice if I just wait long enough. And the Wicked Reform School?

I'd be lucky to survive.

Chapter Six

KING MAXEN

I stand before my mirror as my tailor makes small adjustments to my new black suit. I'm perfection, toned in all the right places and with genetics working on my side, so it only makes sense that my clothes should be as perfect as I am. The expensive material brings attention to the fine cut of every muscle in my body, while still looking eloquent.

It was a hard look to pull off.

As a berserker, the bulk of my people tend to stick to leather and furs, while the vampires prefer suits and the finer things It took a while to create a style that didn't make me look like a bodybuilder squeezed into formal clothes. But now…now even the vampires envied me.

"Very good, Martin," I say.

My tailor stands back. The old shifter's gaze sweeps from the top of my suit to my fine shoes, then he gives a short nod.

A knock at my room draws my attention, and I glance at the door in the reflection of the mirror. "Enter."

Bill enters the room, his face tense. Instantly, my good

mood fades away. When Bill was upset, there was usually a good reason for it. The older berserker comes to stand behind me, his grey hair impeccably styled, just the way I'd instructed he have it styled. And even though there were wrinkles on his sports' coat, it was a massive improvement to the leather vest he wore as my father's advisor.

"What is it?"

His shoulders roll back, as if he's preparing himself for my reaction. "There has been a…problem, with Emory."

A smile touches my lips. Ah, my little step-brother. No matter what I did, he seemed to find trouble wherever he went. Or, perhaps, I found trouble for him just to see if he'd survive.

Kings of old often killed their rivals, knowing that a bastard could easily replace them on the throne. I'd gone a different route with Emory.

The day his mother had shown up at our door, with some story about having hidden the boy from my father but no longer having anywhere to go with him, I'd made a decision. I wouldn't kill him. No, that would be too easy. I'd break him. I'd destroy every fiber of his being and rebuild him to be nothing but a shadow of a man. A solider who followed orders and nothing else.

But that wasn't enough. No matter the situation, he seemed to find admiration. From our people. From my father. From my friends.

Everyone.

And so my plan changed again: not just to break him, but to make it clear to every person who saw him that he was unworthy of even the position of my slave. My hands had been somewhat tied when my father was alive, but the second he died, things got easier.

Now, I ensured he was always going to screw up everything.

And then I proceeded to punish him. Very publically. As often as I could.

"Your highness?" Bill says, his question cautious.

"Tell me of my brother's latest mistake."

The advisor avoids my eyes, something I relished. He'd always met my father's eyes when he spoke, but my father had never truly taught his people how to fear him. Not the way I had.

"The vampires died under his protection."

I stiffen. *Well, that isn't good.* The vampire alpha was a very powerful ally. "His enemies found him…"

"No," he clears his throat, "he was killed by a woman."

"A woman?" I wasn't sure if I should be impressed or angry.

"A woman…who apparently went berserk."

I stare at him. "What did you say?"

"She went berserk, your highness."

A world of possibilities opens up in front of me. So many berserkers were fighting my rule. They called my father cruel. They called me a monster. All because I wanted to unite them under one ruler. All because I wanted to bring berserkers into the twenty-first century and make us as respected as all the other races.

And yet, the berserkers fought me every step of the way. They said I didn't deserve the throne I already sat on and that I'd never earn a throne that ruled over us all.

But every one of us knew the legend. And the leaders of the houses…we knew it was more than just a legend. It was a prophecy. If a berserker male found a female who could go berserk, they would rule over the other houses. They would be made the king and queen.

Even the fucking Lord of the House of Winter Berserkers wouldn't be able to argue against that.

"I'm assuming my brother is bringing her to me?"

Bill stares at his feet. "Your brother and the female are currently arriving at the Wicked Reform School."

"What?" The word drips with outrage.

I step down from the platform and glare at the man. "Do you have any idea what this means? Do you have any idea how important that female is?"

"Yes, Your Highness."

"I want her. Here. Now. No matter the cost."

Bill's gaze lifts but doesn't meet mine. "There are berserkers in the reform school who might be able to be convinced to help us, with the right incentive."

"Give them anything they want, but I want her."

"And your brother?" Bill asks.

I look down at him. What should I do with my brother? I have gotten the idiot out of every situation he's ever been in. I didn't like not having him groveling at my feet. I didn't like having him out of my reach.

And yet…my chest tightens. The female is with my bastard brother. If something were to happen between them, he would be crowned king. He had my father's blood in him. Could I risk freeing them both?

"Enlist my brother's help to free her." I shall decide what I do with him after that.

Bill nods and backs away toward the door. Then his gaze goes to my bed. Three women lie in the sheets…well, the parts of three women lie in the sheets. Most berserkers consider females too precious to harm, but that's because they don't know what it feels like to fuck a woman in their other form. They don't understand the power they hold. They don't know what it feels like to hear the women screaming, to use all their strength to pleasure themselves with a female, alive or dead, it didn't matter.

"Would you like me to…clean them up?"

I look back to my reflection in the mirror and

straighten my tie. "Yes, get everything cleaned. After all, my new bride deserves fresh sheets."

"Very good," he mumbles, then disappears from the room.

"May I go?" my tailor asks.

I look at his pale face, then back at my reflection. "Yes, but I need even more clothes. My bride will expect the perfect husband."

"Of course," he says, bowing his head.

I smile in the mirror. My bride will be perfect. I'll be the perfect husband.

And then, I'll have it all.

Chapter Seven

DRAKE

I sit beneath a tree, eating an apple and regarding the other "students" from beneath my lashes. Today new students were arriving, and apparently, they were headed for the House of Berserkers, named after the most powerful berserker house in all of North America. The instant I'd learned the newbies were berserkers, I'd lost interest.

Berserkers were worse than animals. At least animals made sense. They killed to eat. They fought to survive. And they fucked…well, for fun. But berserkers? They were crazed assholes with a thirst for blood.

I had heard few to none ever made it past the cullings.

Fewer still managed to even survive their time here.

Smiling, I take another bite of my apple. As the fucking berserkers fight amongst themselves, growling and shouting, many of the shifters gather, egging them on. Other students stop to watch the spectacle, at a safer distance, and one of them catches my eye.

A beautiful red-head with a thirst for dragon cock. Too bad for her she isn't my type.

Still, she saunters toward me, casting me sultry looks, then stops to stand in front of me. "Enjoying the sight?" she purrs.

I glance away from her to the fight. "I grow…bored with this place."

She flashes a smile. "Keep being a good boy, and you might actually make it out of here at the next culling."

I huff, a trail of smoke rising from my nostrils. "I doubt it."

Dragon shifters were rare, hunted to the point of near extinction, and if the rest of the supernatural community had their way, we would be extinct. My existence was a thorn in their side. If I didn't screw up on my own, they'd find a way to make me screw up.

Danielle sits down beside me, even though I hadn't invited her to, and trails a hand up my thigh. "Come on, Drake, let's forget about all that."

"Succumbing to my allure again?" I ask, lifting a brow.

She grabs my junk, and I jerk. "I'd want to stroke you off, with or without your lure, baby."

I almost sigh. Dragons are hard to resist. Instinctually, other beings bowed down to my kind, they submitted, and females had an instant desire to mate with us. Compatible females had an even harder time resisting us, but I had a harder time refusing them too. Luckily for me, Danielle was not a compatible mate. Even with her hand working my dick, I stayed limp.

Something she was starting to notice.

"What do you need me to do?" she begs.

"Nothing," I growl. "Find another male."

Instead, she leans closer, and whispers in my ear, "I'll do anything. Fuck my hand, my mouth, my pussy, even my ass. In private. Right here and now, whatever you want, Drake."

Still my dick remains limp. I was a virile male, more than ready to gift a female with my seed, but dragons liked females that were…like treasures, rare and beautiful.

Danielle was not a treasure. She was a woman who confused physical affection with love. A woman who had attached herself to half the men here.

"What do I have to do?" she whispers again.

I try to think of another way to shoot her down gently, but a commotion near the shifters and berserkers distracts me. The security guards are dragging someone in. Someone who seems to be foolish enough to fight back.

For a minute I almost curse the fool. Anyone stupid enough to… And then I see *her*.

I swear the sky opens up. I swear thunder and lightning shake my earth, and my head goes light. The person who fights is a female. A startlingly beautiful female with hair so white it's almost silver. It flows down her strong body, like a curtain that can't possibly protect her from this place. And the leather outfit she wears…a growl explodes from my lips. It reveals far too much of her perfectly curved body. Her large breasts, her tiny waist, her hips made to be grabbed.

"Oh, Drake," I hear Danielle gasp.

I look down and see her working my cock, hard. And the bastard is standing tall and ready.

My gaze moves back to the new woman. The guards have left her, surrounded by the berserkers and shifters. And yet, her eyes are focused on me, specifically on the hand on my cock.

I shove Danielle's hand back and stand. It isn't that I care if my female saw me being touched by another woman. Shifter women understand that a powerful dragon like myself might have many females.

And yet, I will make it clear to this woman that I will

have her as my own.

Crossing out of the shade of the tree, I toss my apple and march across the grass. Already the sounds of the men jeering reaches my ears, and something inside of me twists. She stands in the middle of the big men, and yet there isn't an ounce of fear in her face.

Instead, her small hands bunch into fists.

One of the men grabs her ass. I'm running before I know what I'm doing, and yet before I can reach her, she's knocked him right on his ass, sending the wolf shifter down onto the dirt training area like a tree falling over. I skid to a halt near her.

She's breathing hard. "Anyone touches me…be ready to have your ass kicked!"

There are a few bemused chuckles.

A berserker steps out of the crowd, heading for her, a smirk on his face. He reaches for my female, but I've closed my hand around his throat before I realize I'm moving. His eyes bug out, and I slowly begin to crush the bones in his throat, seeing red.

"Enough!"

I barely register someone has spoken until a small hand touches my arm.

My gaze snaps away from the man and lands on the stunning female. Up close, she's a damned goddess. Lush lips, high cheekbones, dark brows arched over brilliant blue eyes. My heart hammers, and I know I'll need to fuck this woman soon or else lose my mind.

"Put him down," she snaps.

I drop the man and turn toward her. My much larger body dwarfs her smaller one in a way that has me imagining all the ways I could spin this tiny woman on my cock. I lean closer and take a deep breath, breathing in her scent. Instantly, I'm overwhelmed. She smells like nature.

Like the woods, and the water, and the fresh air. But it's more than that. Her scent calls to something within me... the beast within me, in a way no woman has before.

"Come with me," I tell her, my voice low and husky.

I expect many things. For her to allow me to sweep her into my arms. For her to take my arm and walk away.

I do *not* expect the arrogance in her face as she steps back from me. "Not a chance."

A growl builds low in my throat. "Female—"

"I have a name," she snaps.

"Tell it," I snap back.

She gives me a dirty look and then actually turns her back on me and begins to walk away.

Every shifter, every berserker, they stare at us with mouths hanging open. Has any woman ever refused me? Have even the men dared to disobey me?

The answer was simple: no, no they hadn't.

Perhaps this woman was a beautiful, perfectly-scented fool.

"Come back here!" I order, my voice shattering the silence that stretches between us all.

Very slowly she looks back at me, and I have one moment of triumphant before she speaks, "Go to hell, shifter."

A cold hot fury unravels within me. My hands curl into fists. This woman...I will break her. I will make her mine. And when I'm done with her, she will suck my cock on her knees. She will beg for it. She will drink my cum like her favorite snack.

I smile at her, and for the first time I see a flicker of doubt in her eyes.

And then a bell chimes, signaling the first class.

"We'll finish this...later," I promise both her and myself.

Chapter Eight

KIERA

I'm trembling, but I'll be damned if I let the giant shifter know he's gotten to me. But holy hell, I'd have to be a moron not to be scared of him. He was easily seven feet tall, tall even for a damn berserker. Bigger than any berserker I'd met, both in height and size, and that was not an easy feat.

What the hell kind of shifter is he? Not a bear, that was for sure. I'd know a bear anywhere. So what, then? The truth was I had no idea.

But he was also different than any of the men back home. He was…classically handsome, his light brown hair styled, left a little long on top, and his face cleanly shaven. His face was almost too beautiful to be a man's, with green eyes and an almost permanent arrogant expression. He was not at all my usual type, but I felt like a woman who had tasted every flavor of ice cream and was suddenly presented with something entirely new.

Which made me want to beg for a taste.

A shiver moves down my spine. *Why the hell do I find him so damn attractive?*

Berserkers weren't exactly known for holding back when we wanted something. We lived life to the fullest, and because there were so few males, that usually meant we females had multiple partners at any given time. And yet, something about the shifter made me nervous. Maybe it was the way he looked at me like he already owned me. Or the fact that it was hard to breathe when his gaze met mine.

Which meant that even if I wanted to lick every drop of that ice cream cone, I wouldn't. Because the last thing I needed right now was another mysterious man complicating my life.

I ignore the way my thighs clench together, and finally release a breath when the big shifter turns away from me. The two dozen or so people who stand around move to form a circle around a dirt area, but I remain where I'm standing, studying them suspiciously.

A man, who can't be more than a few years older than all of us, comes to stand in the middle of the circle. He crosses big arms over a broad chest and grins. "Who wants to go first today?"

To my surprise, no one volunteers, so I was going to guess whatever he had planned isn't fun.

His gaze sweeps the circle, then falls on me. And the bastard's expression instantly changes. "You must be the new girl."

I glare back at him.

He grins. "Kiera, be a good girl and come here."

I remain where I stand.

Something dangerous flashes in his eyes. "Come here, or I'm going to make you come here, and it's going to be unpleasant."

Every one of the students tense. And I might not be a

genius, but I am an expert at body language. This guy's promise…he means it.

So, carefully, I move toward him.

The students part at my approach, and I continue moving until I come to stand just a foot in front of him. Our teacher looks surprised that I'd drawn so near him. But I know people. If I'm going to do whatever the hell he has planned, I want him to feel deep down that I'm not afraid of him.

"What a good girl," he purrs in a way I find insulting and more than a little creepy. "You know I've never trained a female berserker… I've actually never even met one."

His gaze sweeps to my chest, and I swear I'd never felt grosser. Not only was I wearing the same clothes that I'd been caught in two days earlier, but this asshole is looking at me like he was slowly undressing me.

"Up here, fucker!" I finally say, pointing to my eyes.

His gaze snaps up, and his cheeks heat. "Careful…"

"Careful checking out students," I shoot back at him. "You wouldn't want anyone thinking you're some pervert who takes advantage of the people in your care, because there's a special place in hell for dirtbags like that."

Anger buzzes around him. "You're up next." His gaze snaps to someone in the crowd. "Drake, you're her opponent."

"Opponent?"

The teacher grins. "Why yes, didn't anyone tell you the first class of the day is your training course? Fighting 101, as we like to call it."

"Fighting?" I shrug. Fighting I can do.

I turn slowly around as someone steps free from the circle, and my stomach drops. The massive man I'd insulted just a few moments ago… is currently squaring off with me.

Great, just fucking great.

"So, how does this work? Do we…?"

My opponent roars and dives at me.

If not for a lifetime of training, the fight would've been over right then, but at the last possible second, I twist away. He skids to a halt, whirls around, and his eyes narrow.

"Come on, big boy, come get me."

He dives at me again. This time, I slip to the opposite side, then follow up with a kick to his ass.

The shouting around us dies down to silence.

The big man, this Drake, turns to face me. "That was a mistake."

My hands curl into fists. "Probably not my first one."

He advances on me, going slower this time, and I can tell by the way he advances on me that he'd decided he was done with this game. That he was just going to clock me and end it. I only wonder if he knows I've been fighting big guys my whole life.

Instantly, he swings at me.

I catch his arm and try to pull him forward, to use his momentum against him, but I hadn't been prepared for him to pull his punch at the last possible second. Instead, he leans into me, knocking us both to the ground in an instant.

Struggling, knowing I'm done for if the big guy can pin me, I try to get out from under him. I try to escape, but it's too late. He presses down on me, knocking the air from my lungs. I try to strike him, but he easily catches my wrists, pinning them above my head.

As black edges my vision, I wait for the teacher to call him the victor, but he says nothing.

Drake leans closer and runs his lips along my neck. I shiver as he bites lightly at the junction between my neck and shoulder. Hot need rushes through my body, surprising me, and I'm no longer just gasping from lack of air.

He swears above me, and I feel a shudder wrack his body.

"Hurt her," I hear the teacher command. "Break her. Injure her. Fucking do something, Drake!"

Instead, he lifts his weight from me, if only by a little, then settles between my thighs more comfortably, his erection hard, long, and painfully evident.

My eyes widen. "Get off of me!"

He moves to my ear. "I'm a shifter, sweetheart, I can smell just how wet you are. Want me to take a little taste?"

For one second I consider biting him, and then an idea hits me. I press myself harder against him and whisper, "You better."

His body tenses above me. His weight shifts again, and I'm not sure exactly what he's going to do, but I know he wants me.

I wait for just the right moment, and then I knee him in the groin as hard as I can.

He makes a choking sound above me.

I wiggle a hand free and dive my palm into his nose, then knee him in the groin again before shoving him off of me. When I spring free, I dance away from the giant man and glare at the teacher.

"Are we done now?"

The shifter roars in fury on the ground. I hide my surprise and lift a brow, locking eyes with the teacher. "Are we?"

He shakes himself. "Fine. Done. Go clean up. Next partners, George and Kyle."

I turn my back on all of them, even though I have no idea where the hell I'm supposed to clean up, and head for the closest building. When I reach the steps, I look up at the huge white stone structure. "House of Berserkers" is written across it in black letters.

My mouth curls down. House of Berserkers is also the name of the leaders of all the berserkers in North America. They were run by a bunch of arrogant assholes who were always struggling for more and more power over our clans, even though my father was one of the clan leaders that fought them every step of the way. Living in a building named after them irritated me.

Climbing up the steps, I push open the huge glass doors. On the other side, a man waits. He's thin compared to most berserkers, with blond hair that hangs into his eyes. "Kiera?"

I nod.

"I'm Tyler. I'm sort of in charge of showing newbies around."

"Well, you kind of suck at it," I say. "Those asshole guards dropped me right into that stupid class, and I haven't even gotten a chance to clean up or—" I stop myself. "What I meant to say is thanks, and that I'm not always a bitch, I'm just having a bad day."

His stressed expression fades away. "You'd be surprised by how many people have bad days when they come here."

I smile, and he smiles back.

"Let me show you to your room."

He leads me down the hall to the last room on the first floor. Using a key, he unlocks the door and pushes it open, before handing me the key. I step in, and I'm surprised to find a super small room, but at least a private room.

As my gaze runs over the one bed tucked in one corner, a big window, and a tiny desk, I spot the two familiar bags on my bed. "What's that?" *It can't be.*

"Your family was allowed to send you some belongings," he says, wincing. "The guards take out anything deemed dangerous, but it's still better than an adult prison. We get a little bit of leeway, being youthful criminals and all."

I go to the bags like I'm in a spell and unzip them, breathing deeply of the familiar smells of home. One bag holds clothes. In the other I spot a few pictures, and zip it right back up. If I look at any of that, I'm going to completely lose my shit, and I can't lose my shit in front of this guy.

Then I realize something is under the blanket thrown on my bed. Drawing it back, I spot my axes and gasp. Picking them up, I feel a deep sense of relief that I haven't felt since being taken from my home.

"They let me have these?"

The berserker shrugs. "The angels get their swords. The shifters their teeth and claws. The witches their magic. So, we get our weapons too. But if you kill anyone, be prepared to die in a detention cell."

His mention of a detention cell isn't enough to curb my enthusiasm as I swing them in the air, glorying in the way the perfect blades spin.

"Although," he continues, "I have to say berserkers tend to stick to maces and shit. It's usually only the big guys who use axes."

"These were made for me." By my godfather, and the town blacksmith.

"That explains why they're small enough for you."

"They're big enough to fill my hands, that's usually enough for me."

He blushes. "Well…uh…yeah."

I set them down, find my back sheath, and slide them into the leather. It hurts a little to put them away, but I'm no fool. Sharp things get put away. *How many times had my dad told me that?*

"Can I take a shower and get changed?" I ask.

He nods and pushes open a pocket door beside my bed. "Since you're the only female berserker, we gave you the room with a private bathroom."

"That's…awesome," I say, and actually mean it.

He smiles at me. "Is there anything else?"

"Yeah, uh, what do I do after this?"

He blushes. "Oh yeah, you being a hot girl kind of made me forget the usual routine." He points to my desk. "There's your schedule. Follow it to a T."

"Thanks."

He hesitates as I grab another favorite outfit. "Listen, Kiera?"

"Yeah," I say, stroking the soft leather of my clothes.

"This place…it's not like anywhere you've been before. It's dangerous. So don't get thrown off by the pretty scenery or the school structure. You screw up here, you die. Or worse. And being the only female berserker…well, some of the guys were taught to cherish females like they should, and some…well, some of these guys really deserve their sentence here."

I look up at him and hold his gaze. "I really appreciate the warning."

He nods. "You have twenty minutes, then the next class. Don't be late. Trust me."

"I won't," I promise.

He leaves, and I lock the door behind him. For a minute I just stare at the handle. I want to pretend I'm okay. I want to pretend that none of this matters because I chose this path, but it *does* matter.

I gave up my old life, my freedom, everything…for a strange man. A man who is somewhere at this reform school. I needed to find him and find out why the hell he saved me.

Oh, and avoid the giant, Drake, that I'd made any enemy out of.

And also, apparently, a lot of the men here.

This is going to be fun…oh so fun.

Chapter Nine

EMORY

A guard shoves me along, and I have to fight to keep from going berserk. Anger rolls under my skin, and I have to practice my breathing to keep from changing. I didn't want Kiera anywhere near me. I didn't want her to know who I am and who I'd become.

But something inside me was on edge, driving me mad, pestering me with questions about where she is and why I hadn't seen her. *Was it possible they killed her anyway?* I'd deleted the security recording the moment I'd seen it, but was someone left alive who could tell them who really killed the vampires?

Gods, I hoped not.

When we reach a clearing of trees, I see several students sitting around in a circle. The guard pauses, still too far from them, and calls out, "Go on then to your class, this is as far as I go."

I cast him an annoyed look, but he races out of there like he's trying to outrun a fire. Which wasn't exactly comforting. *What the hell is with these people here?*

Looking back at the group of students, I hear the buzz

of their low voices, but none of them move. They seem to hold themselves strangely still. An instinct sends the hairs on the back of my neck standing on end.

"Be careful, boy."

I stiffen and spin toward the voice.

A man emerges from behind a bush. He's middle-aged for a supernatural, with a bushy brown beard and deeply set dark eyes. He wears a baseball cap so low over his head that his eyes just barely peek out and a loose flannel shirt. In his hand is a rake, and he wears gloves as he rakes the leaves from around the bush.

"Hello, sir," I greet.

"Did you hear what I said?"

He sounds irritated.

"Yeah, but what am I supposed to be careful of?"

He jerks his head toward the class beneath the trees. "That area of the woods belongs to the Myrmidons."

"Myrmidons?" I repeat, frowning.

He rolls his eyes. "Don't you know anything about anything? Myrs are warrior insects."

I can't help the chuckle that explodes from my lips. "Warrior insects? I'm a berserker, so sorry if I'm not shaking in my boots."

He leans on his rake and glares at me. "What are you, stupid? Myrs are dangerous as fucking hell. See all those powerful students in there holding perfectly still? They're trying not to piss the fuckers off. The garden teacher likes to play a game when she's bored. She brings them to the garden and waits to see if a student pisses them off, and the little beasts kill them slowly and painfully."

"Insects?" For some reason I'm having trouble picturing that.

He scoffs. "Yeah, imagine a million ants with swords

and spears, you jackass. Imagine all the insects around you perfectly capable of flaying you to death, very slowly."

That did paint a picture.

"Not so smug now, are you, berserker?"

I incline my head. "Thanks for the warning, sir."

He makes an irritated noise. As he walks away, the sunlight glitters over him for a half a second, and his image grows transparent, then returns to normal.

I'd have to keep an eye out for that guy.

Not wanting to see if the old man's warning was true about the insects, I walk cautiously, watching my every step, as I head for the woods. I see nothing remarkable about the forest, but all the students seem to track my movements with a mixture of fear and awe. So I step carefully, scanning the grass beneath my feet before placing my foot anywhere. It's awkward, but the whole flaying to death image is sort of sticking with me.

When I reach them, the teacher flashes a smile and speaks in a low voice. "Emory, right?"

I nod, immediately feeling on edge. The woman looks nothing like my brother. She has long grey hair left loose around her shoulders. Her skin is wrinkled, and she wears a dress covered in flowers and an apron. And yet, something about her reminds me of him.

Maybe it's just the strange man's warning ringing through my head, but I swear beneath her smile is that same sadistic thirst for pain. It lingers beneath her eyes like a shadow. Everyone who meets my brother thinks he is charismatic, charming, and kind. Hell, I'd thought that too when I first met him.

But then I'd gotten to know him.

And I had the sense that this woman might look like someone's sweet, old grandmother, but that she was a wolf in sheep's clothing.

"Welcome to class," she greets, and she sounds very happy I'm here. *Too* happy. "Join us." She gestures to a spot next to her.

I avoid it and sit down carefully between a couple students.

It's strange. I swear all of the people in her class are terrified. Sweat beads off of several of their foreheads and tears glimmer in one woman's eyes. My gaze runs over everything around me and lands squarely on a place where the grass is tinted red.

My eyes narrow. If I was a shifter, I'd have no doubt that blood lingered in the air.

"Tell us about yourself," she says, again her voice soft.

I match the volume of her voice. "I'm Emory. A berserker. This is my first day."

Long ago I'd learned not to openly rebel against those in power. It was like putting your hand in a fire, you'd just get burnt. But I also learned there were ways to defy people that were more subtle, like telling this woman as little as I could get away with, without seeming openly defiant.

When she realizes that I don't plan to say more, she frowns. "Well, that wasn't interesting." Her head swivels to the woman with tears in her eyes. "Isabelle, tell him about our class."

The woman has short, brown hair and chubby cheeks that give her a youthfulness that's pleasant. I get the feeling that outside of this situation, she's nice to be around. But as she prepares herself to speak, a tear rolls down her cheek. "Ms. Green teaches gardening here at the Wicked Reform School. She feels very strongly that only those of us worthy of reform should survive our class."

"Good," Ms. Green whispers, then licks her lips. "Tell him about today's lessons."

I follow the old woman's gaze and stiffen when I see a creature no bigger than three inches climbing the young woman's stomach and moving to her arm. It's got almost brilliant green skin, a little larger head than the rest of its body, and long arms and long legs. Clutched in one of its tiny hands is a spear, and its large eyes are narrowed as it climbs the woman.

My hand itches to crush the creature in my palm, to ease the fear in the woman's face. But even though berserkers are known for acting first and thinking after, my time spent with my brother had taught me that acting without thinking would get me killed. So, I hold myself back, letting my gaze slide around the woman.

Suddenly, I stiffen. In the spot the teacher had told me to sit, I see the grass move. As my gaze narrows, I spot hundreds of the fucking creatures moving between the blades.

Holy hell, that's not good.

The woman seems to take a minute to collect herself, then continues speaking, even quieter than before. "Today's lesson—"

A man, who wears a cloak with hood pulled down low, interrupts, his expression angry. "Is another chance for her to fucking watch one of us die horribly."

Ms. Green's smile vanished, replaced by an expression of anger. "That was disrespectful, Blake."

The man locks eyes with me. "She chooses the person she wants to break at the beginning of the class. Anyone else is just extra fun."

"Tisk, tisk, tisk," Ms. Green whispers. "Kids nowadays have no respect. But then, that's what led you here, vampire, right?"

His jaw clenches, but he says nothing else.

She moves her hand in a slow gesture, and the tension

within the students increases. Suddenly, plants push through the earth around us and sprout forth, growing at a rapid pace. Bright green vines curl around us as we sit, almost trapping us in the clearing. Some of the little creatures are disturbed. An angry chattering comes, not just from the ones on the ground, but from every bush and tree around us.

I swallow hard, my gaze darting around the woods surrounding us, then back to the teacher.

She slowly drops her hand. "I think today is as good a day as any to clean out the class."

The young woman makes a strange sound, and I look back at her to see the little Myrm has reached her shoulder. It climbs the slight folds of her neck and clings to her ear, before swinging himself up. My heart races as the creature looks into her ear, then slowly pushes its way in.

Suddenly, she screams and shakes her head, then tries to dig into her ear.

My mouth opens in a warning.

Her eyes widen, and then roll back into her head. She falls backwards. The second she hits the ground, she's no longer breathing. Thousands of the creatures flood over her, and I look away as they use their weapons to stab at her flesh. Women were precious. Women were worth dying for. But this woman was already gone.

This place is fucking twisted.

The teacher stares at her with rapture. Her eyes seem to glow with pleasure, and she slowly licks her lips. I've seen a lot of disturbing things, but even I feel sick to my stomach.

"May we go?" the vampire asks.

Ms. Green answers with a distracted nod.

We all rise slowly and carefully make our way back out of the forest. When we reach the grass where the sunlight reaches, another woman begins to cry and takes off. A man barfs into a nearby bush, and I stare at them all, feeling uneasy.

Is this what all the classes will be like at Wicked Reform School?

"I'm Blake," the vampire says, holding out his hand.

Vampires aren't exactly my favorite paranormals, but we're both here, so I shake his hand. His grip is tight, and his dark eyes, ringed by red, watch me carefully. When he releases my hand, I start back toward the largest building on campus, even though I have no idea where I'm going.

"Did they run through your schedule and all that shit?"

I shake my head.

"Yeah, they don't care enough to do more than dump us here. The guide for the House of Berserkers should have the info for your room assignment and shit, if you can even find him."

I grunt in response.

We continue walking in silence, but I sense he has more to say. But then, vampires always have more to say. My brother thinks having the bastards in his home will make people see us as more than brutes, but he doesn't seem to understand that vampires are just well-dressed beasts, not so different from us at all.

But without souls.

"Your brother wasn't happy about you being sent here."

I stiffen, then move without thinking, grasping him by the shirt and dragging him closer. "What the fuck did you just say?"

He looks shocked. "I heard some people discussing it."

I shake him. "What did they say?"

He swallows hard. "They said he wasn't happy, and that they were going to get to the bottom of you. And the woman."

I feel sick, but then, I shouldn't be surprised. My brother has spies everywhere. He'll have heard about Kiera and about what I did. I'd kind of hoped being imprisoned might protect both of us from him.

Guess I was wrong.

"That's all I know. I swear!"

I drag him a little closer. "Say nothing about what you heard to anyone. Understand me?"

He nods, really fast.

"Now, take me to where I can find my guide," I order him, then shove him back.

"Fuck," he mutters, straightening his shirt. "You could've just asked."

Maybe I could have. But now that I know my brother has men here, I have to find Kiera. And soon. Or she might be in more danger than she ever imagined.

Chapter Ten

KIERA

*B*efore I could start my next class, I was called to the dean's office. Which I was going to assume was a bad thing. A uniformed man leads me through the center of the Wicked Reform School, instead of around the outside path like the guard that had brought me here. And since this uniformed man is quiet, and not relentlessly pushing me forward, I take the time to look around.

I'm surprised to find that passed the House of Berserkers, and the collection of training grounds, there's a main part of the campus. It's a collection of large buildings, spread out, with plants and trees weaving through them. Several fountains give a strangely soothing, almost elegant feel to a place that's little more than a dressed-up prison.

The silent man takes me to the huge building in the center of it all, and up two flights of stairs. Outside of a door, he raps in a strangely rhythmic way, then opens the door. He holds it open for me, then follows in after.

In a monotone voice, he tells a young secretary, "Kiera of the House of Berserkers."

The pretty blonde turns to me and flashes a big smile, her voice sweet as she says, "Hi, Kiera. Just take a seat!"

I eye her and the quiet man, then seat myself on some soft green couches.

She picks up a phone and hits a button. "Hi, Dean Aero, this is Ms. Natalia Brevins." She pauses, then giggles. "Oh yeah, don't introduce myself every time, I remember." Another pause. "Why *was* I calling?" She frowns.

I lift a brow and wave at her.

Her brown eyes lock onto mine. "Oh yeah, she's here!" Another pause. "Kiera, the berserker." Then, "Yes, sir. Thank you sir. Okay, I'll remember to hang up." She sets the phone down and beams at me.

I stare back.

Then she looks at the silent man still at the door. "You can go, Henry."

He leaves, closing the door behind him.

She's back to beaming at me. "I'm a golem."

I blink slowly. "I'm sorry?"

"Sorry for what?"

I stare. *Is she serious?* "I meant, I'm sorry, I don't understand the golem thing."

"Don't worry about it! There's a lot I don't know! Because I'm a golem. The Dean of Discipline created me to help run his office. Actually, he helped create most of the staff. I mean, the guards are mostly other beings, because they need more freewill to make quick decisions. But most of the staff are actually made, rather than born. Like me."

Okaaay. "So you were made…"

"Like a doll." She beams at me and stands up. She moves around her little desk. She's wearing a tight pencil skirt and pink high heeled stilettos. She doesn't wear a bra, and I'm kind of surprised by how tight and see-through her top actually is. "See," she spreads her arms out on both sides of herself, "Dean Aero made me into the perfect secretary!"

Already I don't like this Aero guy.

Suddenly, the door leading into his office opens. A tall man, wearing a neat blue suit and a tie that's slightly askew, steps into our room. He has a look of barely concealed annoyance on his face, but like he's trying really hard not to look angry.

I tense, but the secretary just spins around on those tall shoes of hers. "Hi, Dean, I was just telling her about being a golem and your perfect secretary."

"Yes, well." He clears his throat.

She moves to him and fixes his tie. "There, perfect."

"I thought you were going to send her in."

The secretary's bottom lip sticks out and begins to tremble. "I remembered to hang up the phone."

He sighs and smacks her ass, hard. "It's okay, sweetcheeks." Then, he turns to me. "Kiera…why don't you head into my office."

I climb to my feet and smooth down my clean clothes. I'm glad I had time to shower before being dragged here. My new outfit has tall, comfortable black boots. Black, luxurious leather pants that are soft and smooth, not that shiny, gross leather, hug my legs like a second skin. And my black tank top fits snuggly and dips low in the back.

My second favorite outfit.

I walk past them, my long blonde hair still damp and hanging down my back. Entering his office, I'm surprised by how bright the room is. Big windows look down at the courtyard and the massive fountain in the center. The room is decorated like it came out of a "Modern Stuff Today" magazine, with only black and white furniture and accessories.

I frown. It doesn't have a drop of fur, leather, or touches of earth colors. So basically, just the kind of place any berserker would hate. I sit down in a white chair that faces the big black desk, with a clear plastic chair. Out in the secretary's room, I hear her giggle, and what sounds like him slapping her ass again.

To say I found the whole "create a perfect secretary with big tits and a tiny waist thing" a little gross was an understatement. I only hoped that the golem had some kind of freewill. The thought of him using her like his own personal blow-up doll was creepy as hell.

Dean Aero walks back into the room and closes the door behind him, then crosses the room and seats himself across from me. "So, Kiera, you're better-looking than I imagined."

Definitely a creep.

"Thanks," I say, wrinkling my nose.

"I've been reviewing your file and trying to decide if you were going to be some hulking man-like berserker. And I have to say, I find muscular women a bit disgusting."

You mean you're intimidated by them, asshole. "How nice," I say, biting back my desire to add, *you tiny-dicked womanizer*.

"So then, let's talk. Your file says they weren't sure whether or not you killed a room full of vampires. Given your tiny stature, and your lack of muscles or magical abilities, I'm going to go out on a limb and say you weren't responsible for what happened in that room."

My teeth clench together, and it takes me a minute to relax my jaw enough to speak. "I said I killed them, so I killed them."

His eyes narrow. "Are you…mixed?"

"Mixed?"

"A mutt of some sort."

I bristle. "I am Kiera. My father is Lord of the Winter Berserks, and my mother is Lady of the Winter Berserks."

He doesn't look impressed. "So just a purebred Berserker. A female. A nothing."

"I am not a nothing," hisses past my lips.

"So then…you went berserk?"

"I didn't," I lie.

He leans forward, lowering his voice. "I need the truth from you, Kiera, and the truth might very well set you free."

I draw myself up taller, and notice the way his eyes go to my chest. "I am Kiera of the Winter Berserkers, and I'm dangerous, as a female berserker alone. I do *not* need to go berserk to be dangerous."

"And yet if you could go berserker, the House of Berserkers has a deal for you."

I say nothing, just stare.

His voice lowers further. "I can expunge your record and send you out of here, today, if you agree to be the bride to King Maxen of the House of Berserkers. You would be the queen to all the berserkers. You would have unimaginable wealth and privilege…"

I lift a brow, completely unimpressed. "You're aware that the only one that calls that asshole "king" is Maxen himself and his followers. He might be the lord of the largest berserker house, but that doesn't mean he's *our* king."

He laughs. "Are you stupid, girl? I realize you come from the Winter Berserkers, and you guys have a whole thing about your independence, but surely even you realize that this is your get-out-of-jail free card. Right?"

This guy is a moron if he thinks being the wife to that asshole is better than being here. I'd never met him before, but my father ranted about him after every council meeting. Maxen felt that his voice should count for more because he ruled over more berserkers. Some of the council members agreed. But many of the lords, like my father, didn't want the bloodthirsty monster ruling any of them.

I could only imagine how miserable the people in his lands were. I'd heard he ran things like a dictatorship. His word was law. And anyone who spoke up against him ended up dead.

"Like I said, I didn't go berserk," I say, emphasizing each word.

His eyes narrow. "You realize that surviving here isn't guaranteed. And that berserkers almost never make it to the cullings."

Ah, yes. The cullings. An Enforcer had explained the basic details of the school on my ride here. Cullings happened almost at random at the school, while the big ones were at the end of each "term." Certain students were evaluated. Those that were deemed reformed were set free. Those that were deemed incapable of reforming were killed.

It sounded like a good time…

"I'm not worried about it," I lie.

"Well, I guess if you don't go berserk, you should be okay. But if you were lying to me…and you loose control here, well, that would pretty much sign your death certificate."

My heart races, and I actually feel my body start to swell for a horrifying moment before I push my fears and frustrations aside and gain control of myself again. "I understand," I say, sounding breathless.

He scowls at me and waves me away. "Go. Get out of my sight. Apparently, I have King Maxen to call."

I rise.

His next words are soft. "But don't be surprised if those that are loyal to him make things very hard for you around here."

Hell, did I really just make such a powerful enemy? I open my mouth to say more, but I glance out the window and stiffen. Near the fountain, the man who saved me is being dragged down the path by four men…shifters or berserkers, I couldn't tell for sure.

"Thanks," I mumble, then rush out of the room.

In the waiting room, the secretary leaps to her feet. "Do I need to call Henry to come get you, or do you know where to go?"

"I got it," I say, sprinting from the room.

I rush down the hall, half-run down the stairs, and explode out of the building, glancing toward where I saw the man who saved me. But he's no longer there. I try not to look suspicious as I jog after him. When I leave the courtyard, I see him and the four men turn a corner between a collection of small buildings.

Rushing after them, I turn the corner and stop short. The alley just…ends.

Where the hell did they go?

I walk slowly around it, touching all the walls, touching all the stones. The only thing I can imagine is that there's a secret room or a secret passageway, but I find nothing. When I circle back, my foot comes down on a gate. Frowning, I look down. It's big enough for the giant berserkers to climb through. But is that the direction they went?

Kneeling down, I lift the grate, and it easily opens on hinges. *Hinges on a grate? That's not normal.*

Below the grate, there's just darkness and the sound of water dripping. I nibble my bottom lip. Dropping through some dark sewer grate is just the kind of thing I'd normally want to do, to follow some strange man who'd saved my life, but then Lucy was around to tell me not to be an idiot.

I feel tears sting my eyes. Hell, every time I thought of her it felt like someone had punched me in the gut, but I couldn't do anything to bring her back. But I *could* follow the guy who had saved me and make sure he wasn't in trouble because of me.

Taking a deep breath, I let my muscles tense, then jump into the darkness below. For a second I'm simply falling into nothingness, and then I hit the ground, falling perfectly. Rising to my feet, I give a silent prayer of thanks for all my years of training, then peer into the darkness. For several long seconds I can't make anything out, and then my eyes adjust.

I'm in the center of a big tunnel. One way leads into shadows. The other way is lighted every so often by what I imagine is the outside light leaking in through the slits of grates. My ears strain to pick up any sounds. Anything that might tell me what way to go. But all I can make out is the slow dripping of water.

And then I hear it. Low talking. Feet splashing through the couple of inches of water on the tunnel ground.

Turning in the better-lit direction, I start walking. Completely unaware of what I'm walking into. Years of training means that even though I move through water, I mostly keep my feet from splashing. I wasn't silent, but I was as close to silent as a person could be, creeping through a disgusting sewer tunnel.

For a time, I just kept moving. Every time there is a divide ahead, I hesitate, listening until I hear a sound that I think might indicate people ahead. Slowly, the tunnels seem to open up. I'm able to step out of the water onto one of two concrete paths that line each side of the water. The tunnel curls downward. Less light reaches this part of the tunnels, but small red lights also begin to line the path, casting everything in an eerie scarlet glow.

I'm so preoccupied trying to take in my surroundings, that when I hear a loud voice far too close up ahead, I only have a minute to flatten myself against the wall or risk being seen. Breathing hard, heart racing, I cling to the wall for far too long. Watching. Waiting. Wondering if the loud voice just a few feet in front of me, just around the next bend, will take a few steps back and find me.

And I wonder what will happen if I'm seen.

But slowly, the low talking begins again, and I listen as the steps continue once more. A light flashes on somewhere ahead of me, and I inch around the corner and peer ahead of us. It takes a long second for my eyes to adjust to the brightness again, but then I spot the men, including the berserker who had saved me. One of the men slides aside one of the concrete walls to reveal a hidden room beyond.

I duck back, afraid one of them might turn and spot me, and count to ten before looking again.

All the men are gone.

Creeping forward, I reach where the concrete wall has been opened and peek inside.

To my shock, I discover a massive room that screams of a guys' hang out. Big televisions sit on nearly every wall, along with couches. One side of the room is set up like a gym, with weapons hanging off the walls. On the other side is a bar, complete with snacks.

What the hell?

The strange berserker who saved me is shoved into a chair that faces me. The other men take their seats on a big couch that faces him, their backs to me, and one man sits on a large chair across from the strange berserker.

At last, the strange berserker sighs. "What do you want, Mario?"

The dark-haired man in the chair across from him grins. "You know what I want."

He leans back, looking casual, even though I can sense the tension in his movements. "I've said everything I need to say."

Mario grins and reaches for a bottle of liquor on a small table next to him. He pours two glasses of the dark liquid and hands one to my bearded berserker. The berserker takes the drink, but I notice he waits to sip from it until Mario does.

The other man smiles. "We just want to know the truth about the female."

"I already told you. She was just in the wrong place at the wrong time. I got angry with the vampires and snapped."

Mario laughs. "I've seen what your brother has put you through. I've watched you whipped and beaten. I've watched you burnt, spit on…hell, I've watched him urinate on you. And you never broke. So what the hell did the vampires do that made you snap? Huh?"

He sips his drink slowly and runs a hand through his dark hair. "Does it matter?"

Mario leans forward and even I can sense the unspoken threat in his movements. "You know what I think? I think you're protecting her…because of the prophecy. And if you are, I want you to know it's a mistake."

Is he? My stomach twists. I hadn't had time to think about all this prophecy shit, but I knew for a fact that no man was going to marry me and suddenly fart out a crown. It was something made up by bored people. And yet, logic wasn't going to save me.

Or, apparently, the bearded berserker.

"I'm not protecting her."

"You better not be, because your brother has a new job for you."

My berserker stiffens. "I'm locked up here. I'm not getting out any time soon."

Mario grins. "Your new job is to get the female to the school gates. He'll get you out from there. Then your brother will test her. If she goes berserk, he'll marry her. If she doesn't, he'll kill her. But either way, you'll be free."

A chill moves beneath my skin, and I feel every hair on my body stand on end.

Mario's grin fades. "Emory, you know damn well that King Maxen will have her if he wants her, with or without your help."

Emory. The name of my best friend from childhood echoes through my mind. Surely this man is another Emory…the name is uncommon, but this can't be him.

My gaze runs over the massive berserker, his face covered in a wild beard. My eyes lock onto his uncommon blue eyes, a deep blue that almost seems impossible. The same deep blue as the little boy who held my hand, who laughed easily and promised me his heart.

Emory…it can't be him.

My stomach lurches, and I feel bile rise up. *Emory was the brother of Lord Maxen of the House of Berserkers? The same Lord Maxen who wanted me as a bride?* No, it couldn't be.

Could it?

"What do you say, Emory? Will you serve your king?"

I hold my breath.

Emory slams the rest of his drink and sets his cup down on the table next to him, his eyes dead. "I live but to serve my king."

No. I take a step back, then another. The man who saved me was my enemy. The man who saved me was the boy I grew up with. If these people found me here, would they rush me right out? Would they serve me up to the king like some kind of non-virgin sacrifice?

Suddenly, my foot sloshes loudly into the water as it leaves the concrete path, the sound loud in the silence. Every head turns slowly toward me, and Emory's eyes widen as they fall on me. Time stands still, and then Mario shouts, "Get her!"

I turn and start running, but in my frantic state I take a wrong turn. I slam into the dead end, hitting the stone hard, before realizing that I was screwed. Turning back around, I hear the footsteps of the men.

My heart races, and I bunch my hands into fists, knowing there's nowhere left to run, and also knowing that I'd rather die in these dark tunnels then be turned over to be the bride of my enemy. My heartbeat fills my ears. I count the last seconds before I have to fight a group of male berserkers.

A fight I have no chance of winning.

And then a hand wraps around my mouth and pulls me into the darkness.

The stone wall closes once more in front of me, and I'm suddenly trapped in the darkness, sandwiched between stone and a hard body. Hot air breathes onto my throat, and fear squeezes my soul.

My enemies are on the other side of the wall.

A stranger holds me captive in the dark.

What should I do? And will either choice save my life?

I doubted it.

Chapter Eleven

ADAM

I should kill the woman. Even though she smells of flowers. Even though her hair is the color of purity and goodness. She comes from above. She will hurt me, beat me, be cruel to me.

She is one of them.

It would take nothing at all to snap her neck.

And yet, her body feels small and fragile pressed up against me. Feminine and soft. And as much as I want to curse the smell…not just of flowers, but of earth and leather, it tickles my nostrils in the most pleasant of ways.

I'm surprised when I feel my cock harden. *Has it ever hardened before?* I frown, trying to imagine a time when it could have done such a thing, but my memories are filled with pain and torture.

Hard cocks are for pleasure…and I'd certainly never felt pleasure before in my life.

I lean down and taste the skin of her throat. She shudders before me, and I continue to taste her neck, drinking in her scent. Drinking in the softness of her skin beneath my lips. I bite lightly and feel her shudder again.

Does she like what I do? Or is it fear that makes her react so?

Females find me frightening. Disgusting. Strange and unworthy. Likely this woman of brightness and flowers feels the same, and yet, I don't release her. My hand stays across her mouth, and I hear the sounds of the fucking berserkers on the other side.

Does she know I saved her life? Does she know that the men who were chasing her wanted her blood? I don't know. Always there are so many questions and so few answers.

"You're sure she went this way?" a harsh voice asks.

The woman in front of me trembles. *Does she think I will reveal her?* Perhaps. But I never would. Not just because some strange instinct made me save her, but because I would have to reveal myself too.

The berserkers are killers of anyone they find in these tunnels. Even though these tunnels belong to me.

I run my lips against her neck again and feel her soften against me. It's not a response I'd ever expect from a woman. Not one that I touch.

I'm curious if the woman reacts to me out of fear or pleasure. For some reason, it's very important to me to know. In the tunnels, I hear and see many things. I've witnessed sex. Fast sex. Slow sex. Hard sex. Soft sex. I've learned many things, things that never mattered to me before, before when my cock remained soft.

Letting my free hand trail her arm, I run it across her belly, then lift her shirt to touch the soft skin there. At last she tries to look back at me, but I know it's too dark for her eyes to see me. But my eyes…my eyes see her.

I've never thought a woman was beautiful before, but this woman…I finally understand beauty. Her face has pleasant curves. Her eyes are big and wide, and I know the lips beneath my hand are full.

Suddenly, I drop my hand. She's breathing hard; her breath is hot on my face.

My mind drifts back to every time I've seen a woman and man this close. It always led to kissing. Does she expect it from me now? And if I do it, how will I know if I've done it right?

I let my lips caress hers, very gently, slowly, trying to watch her reactions to know if I'm pleasing her. Kissing has always confused me. It seemed a strange thing to press mouths together, but now I understand. Her lips seem to awaken nerves I didn't know existed.

Men on the other side of the wall curse. I'm certain they've been pushing along the walls, trying to find the entrance to these tunnels. I almost smile. They will never find them. They might think they rule the darkness, but only I know the truth.

"We'll find her," a deep voice says, and the woman stiffens.

A low growl builds in the back of my throat. *Who is this man to make the woman react so? Does he hurt her the way my creators hurt me?*

"I'll catch her, and I'll do as the king asked."

My ears strain as the men walk away. The woman wiggles against me, and I realize that I'd been holding her too closely, and let my grip ease.

"Who are you?" she whispers.

"Adam." The word comes out gravelly with misuse.

"I'm Kiera," she says, and I drink in the musical quality of her voice. "Thank you."

"For what?" I rasp.

"Saving me."

"Who said I saved you?" I study her face, my unique vision separating her face from the darkness. "I haven't decided yet."

Her breathing picks up, and I watch the rise and fall of her breasts with fasciation. The hand under her shirt moves higher, and I cup one of her breasts.

"What are you doing?"

It's my turn to shudder. I hadn't thought about it before I acted. My body seemed to have a mind of its own. "I don't know. I've never wanted a woman before. My cock has never grown hard for a woman."

"Never?" She sounds doubtful.

"Never."

"So you're a virgin?"

I think over her question. Virgin. I know this word. "Yes."

"I want to see you," she says, and there's a breathless quality to her words.

I drop my hand from her breast. Once she sees me, she'll know what I am. She'll hate me like the others. She'll find me disgusting, or even fear me. I don't want her to see me.

"No."

"Why not?"

I close my mouth. I won't explain it to her. "Why do you need to see me?"

"I just…I just do."

"Can we not be friends if you don't know what I look like?"

She takes a minute to speak. "It doesn't seem like you want to be friends. Maybe something else."

Something else. I ponder that. I ponder what it means to be friends and something else. Perhaps she's right; I don't want to be friends. I want to touch her. I want her to touch me. And I want to see if my hard cock can do more.

"Adam…" I've always hated the name my creators

gave me, but I like the way she says it. "Is there somewhere else you can take me?"

"You don't like it here?"

"It's dark…and cramped."

Ah, most creatures don't like the darkness or the way the tunnels hug us. This I can understand. This I can fix for the strange woman.

Turning her to face me, I place my hands on her hips and lift her. Automatically her legs wrap around my back, and she gasps slightly.

"Hands around my neck," I order her, but my words come out strangely low.

She does as she's told. "Do you…have to carry me like this?"

I pull her closer, and I'm shocked at the wave of desire that moves through me as my cock presses between her thighs. My head spins ever-so-slightly, and my mouth goes dry. *Carrying her this way makes sense, so why does it feel so good?*

"Why?" I rasp.

She lets out a slow breath. "Adam, this feels…I can feel just how hard you are."

"So?" I ask, then begin to carry her through the tunnels.

I've never carried someone before. But now, now I've realized it might be better to have her on my back. And yet, the arousal that uncurls within me with each step I take is enough for me to keep her in front of me, her legs curled around my back.

In fact, the faster we move, the more she rubs against my erection. I grasp her upper thighs and bounce her against me, gasping in breath at just how good it feels.

We're halfway to my home when I feel my balls tighten. I freeze and turn in the tunnel. Acting on instinct,

I rub against her harder and harder, then feel my seed spill into my boxers.

My head spins, and my legs tremble, when I realize she's rubbing herself against me ever-so-slightly. I hold myself, amazed. *Does she find me attractive too? Does this arouse her too?*

"Kiera," I pant her name.

She stops.

"Come."

"I—I—I don't even know who you are."

"Adam," I remind her.

A low chuckle that makes my cock hard again comes from her lips. "I don't just…come with anyone."

For some reason, her words irritate me. Of course I am not a man she would come with. Not this woman who smells of flowers and the earth.

Not any woman.

I continue to carry her, frustrated by the way my cock continues to stay hard. Frustrated by just how good it feels as I rub between her legs. I will myself not to come again, but I know so little about arousal and my body. *Will I even have a choice when it hits me again?*

"So who are you?" she asks.

"Adam," I repeat again, feeling angry.

Her hand strokes the back of my neck, and I freeze, shocked by how good the touch feels.

"I didn't know touch could feel good," I say, the words springing from my lips.

Her hand stops.

"You can keep going," I tell her, instantly missing her touch.

She continues to stroke my neck, and the hairs stand on end. "Touch should always feel good."

I continue walking, dark memories unraveling in my

mind. "Not when they're hurting me. Not when they're cutting, poking, kicking, hitting. No, touch never feels good."

She surprises me by drawing closer, her head resting on my chest. "I'm so sorry, Adam."

No one has ever said they felt sorry for me. I'm not sure how I should feel.

I push aside a wall and click it back into place behind me. I do the same thing with two more walls, then come to the secret passageway leading to my home. Here she will see me. Here she will know the truth.

The urge to turn around and go back unleashes inside of me. But for some reason, I've changed my mind. I *want* her to see me. I want her to know.

Then I will see that she's like all the others. I can snap her neck, or drag her back to the surface. And all of this… my hard dick…the way her scent fills my nose…all of it will seem like a dream.

Taking a deep breath, I push open the secret passageway and the golden glow of the crystals spill out into the dark tunnels. My home is connected to the sewers, but it is part of the caverns that run beneath the school. Here, the water is clean and pure, running from the mountains far away. Here, the magic crystals give light and warmth. And the special plants that grow beneath give off a glow that fill the space.

I step inside and slide the door closed behind me. The woman moves as if to climb down, but my hands tense on her hips, and she settles against me once more. "This is your home? It's beautiful."

I let my gaze sweep over the large cavern. The golden crystals bathe everything in a surreal light. Flowers that glow the same color grow from the floor. A river flows through one part of the cavern before disappearing further into the earth. My bed, a sewn platform of the velvety soft grass that grows, sits in the center of the room, and a woven blanket lies on top.

This place has always been special to me, but I never imagined anyone else might think it was beautiful. Hell, I never imagined showing it to anyone else. *So why did I show it to the strange woman?*

I turn to look at her and find her staring, openmouthed.

My mind stops. She's just as beautiful in the light as she was in the dark, maybe even more so, with her white-blonde hair cascading down her shoulders and back, and the brilliant color of her blue eyes revealed beneath the crystals' light.

But now she knows. Now she has seen me.

I squeeze my eyes closed, not wanting to see the look on her face. Not wanting to see the moment that she realizes that it was a mutant that saved her. A mutant who kissed her.

"Adam?"

It's hard to speak with the pain radiating from my chest. "Yes?"

"You never said you were so handsome."

My eyes flash open. *Is she serious?* She looks serious. "I'm a mutant."

A mutant with long, tangled blond hair. Not the color of bright gold like hers, a pale shade that's weaved with brown. And my eyes… they're golden and glow at times, telling the world what I am. A bright color that I can't hide, no matter how much I try.

"Oh, Adam, I'm so sorry."

Sorry. That word again that no one says. "Sorry for what?"

She runs her hand along my cheek. "Sorry for everything you went through. I know how they make mutants. I know what they do, and I…"

"Don't," I say. "I don't want to think about that now."

"Then what do you want?" Her gaze drifts to my lips, and I'm surprised by the urge to kiss her again.

"I want to kiss you. I want to fuck you."

Her eyes widen. "Adam…"

"Do you want that?"

Her cheeks turn red. "Well, I have to admit, you're…I mean, you're hot. And for some reason, I, I don't know."

I frown. "I don't know how to court a woman. I don't understand any of this. What do you want?"

She tilts her head and studies me. "You're really a virgin?"

I nod. *Why does she think I'd lie about that?*

"Bring me to your bed."

I obey her, still confused by what she might want. *Will she tell me in the bed? Or is she too tired to speak about it?*

I lay her down, still on top of her, and her legs remain wrapped around my back. My cock aches in my boxers, and she slides her hands from around my neck to the muscles of my bare chest.

"Adam…"

My balls harden at the sound of my name on her lips. All I want is to have sex with her. To do some of the things I've seen and decide why I find her and no other woman attractive. And yet, I need a signal. I need to know what she wants.

"Yes?"

She looks up at me and squeezes her legs around me harder.

I'm panting, overwhelmed with desire. *Does she know when she squeezes me like that my dick rubs even harder between her thighs? Does she know that she's only making the feeling inside of me more uncontrollable?*

"Adam…" she repeats my name again, sounding frustrated.

I look down at her breasts, wanting to taste them. Wanting them in my mouth. If only she would tell me what to do.

She slides her hands between us and grabs my cock.

A string of curses leaves my lips. This damned woman needs to tell me what she wants. Before my cock spills its seed again. *Doesn't she realize what touching me like this is doing?*

She lifts a brow.

I stare down at her in frustration.

She slowly runs her hand along my length.

Finally, I snap. "I want to have sex with you, but what the hell do you want?"

A musical laugh leaves her lips. "I'm in your bed… stroking your dick."

"So you do realize it!"

Her laugh comes again. "Adam, this is how a woman shows you that she wants to have sex with you."

I freeze. "You mean, this is a yes for sex?"

Instead of answering, she leans up, tangles her fingers through my hair, and pulls me down for a kiss. This time, the kiss isn't some gentle tasting. It's hard. It's demanding. And her tongue even slips into my mouth, causing a whole new kind of pleasure.

When at last our kiss breaks, I look down at her in desperation. "So, yes for sex?"

The damned woman only laughs again. Then she pushes me back onto the bed. Standing, she removes her shirt, revealing a bra that does little to hide her perfect breasts. She strips off her boots and pants, then stands before me in nothing but a tiny black pair of underwear and a matching bra.

My erection strains so damned painfully that I actually think I might lose my mind.

"Woman…what do you want me to do?"

She grins. "Alright, Adam, let me make this very clear. I want to have sex with you. Right now. I'm going to show you what to do, and you're going to like it."

I settle back on the bed, my muscles relaxing. *Finally. Was that so damn hard?*

Chapter Twelve

KIERA

It's true that berserkers like sex. It's true that we have no qualms about one-night stands and fucking someone just because we have an itch that needs to be scratched. But this whole situation is strange, even for me.

The thing is, within seconds of being trapped between that wall and this man, I'd found myself unexplainably aroused. If I was a shifter, I'd have thought he smelled like my mate. But it wasn't a scent. It wasn't even that he'd felt deliciously muscular behind me, or that his hard cock against my back had made my own juices flow.

It was…something I couldn't put my finger on.

I stare down at him, not exactly surprised that I'm finding it hard to control myself with him. He's…remarkably handsome. With long, dirty-blond hair, he looks like some kind of wild creature. But the cut of his face is so damn beautiful, rugged in all the best ways possible. And his eyes? They're the unique gold color of most mutants.

How had this man ever thought he was some freak?

Every woman in my town would have jumped his bones and taught him just how to use that massive dick of his…and it was massive. Berserkers were big guys, but I'd known he was packing something special just from the way his tent pole was rubbing between my thighs.

Now, I was slick with desire, staring down at his boxers with a mixture of awe and curiosity. Linking a finger into the front of them, I pull the material off and my jaw drops open. *Holy hell, a gorgeous virgin with a long, thick dick.*

I must have hit my head in the tunnels. I must be dreaming this whole damned thing.

I clean the cum off his erection, then pull the rest of the material down his legs and drop them on the ground. "You sure you want this?" I ask him.

His gaze slides over me. "I've never wanted a woman before, but I think I need you. I think I might die if we don't fuck."

"Well then…" I trail off.

Being told that he needs to fuck me or die is just about the nicest compliment I've ever had from a man. I strip my bra and underwear off, and he makes a sound of arousal. Staring down at him, I realize how much all of this must be new to him. Hell, he'd been surprised that touch could bring pleasure.

I'm going to kill whoever made him think that way. The thought surprises me, and I try to push it aside as I crawl over him.

"What do you want?" I ask him, the question surprisingly husky.

"I want to experience…everything. I want to touch and taste every part of you." His eyes burn into mine. "Before you're gone and I'm alone again."

I'm shocked by the pain in his voice. I stroke the

stubble on his glorious face and almost tell him he'll never be alone again. But I won't make a promise I might not be able to keep. Instead, I kiss him, slowly and gently, then go back to tangling my tongue with his.

He seems to drink in every second of it. His arms are at his side, as if he's surrendered to me.

When I break our kiss, his eyes are locked onto me. "Touch can feel good."

I run my hand down his chest, then wrap my fingers around his length. "I'm going to show you just how good."

I pump him, amazed by the way he looks at me, as if memorizing my face. Then I move lower, still working his cock, and press kisses along his throat and chest. I try to pretend not to notice the deliberate scars that cover nearly every inch of his flesh, but they're impossible to ignore. My heart aches at the pain he must have endured at the hands of his creators.

But I'm also determined to do everything in this moment to make him forget, at least for a few minutes, all his pain and heartache. When I come to his cock, I don't hesitate before slipping him into my mouth.

He groans above me. "That's…amazing."

I suck him slowly and gently, still using my hand to work him. Following the lead of his body, I suck him deeper and slide up and down his impressive length faster and faster until he makes a strangled sound and comes into my mouth.

Oh holy hell. I'm shocked by the flavor of his cum. It's… delicious, like ice cream. I don't even know what I'm doing when I realize that I'm licking the bastard clean.

Is this some kind of mutant thing? I'd thought they were trying to make the perfect creature. *Who knew they were trying to make delicious cum?*

He's laying back, his expression shocked, when I rise up between his thighs. "How was that?"

"That was…that was…there are no words."

I grin, trying to ignore the way my pussy throbs as I look down at him. *Can the guy go again?* Hell, I could take him all day long and still want more, but he's inexperienced. Either he'll be drained, or he'll have a lifetime of pent-up desire to spare.

Silently, I hope for the second one.

Climbing on top of him, I spread over his dick and let him rub in my juices. I'm shocked when it only takes him seconds to harden, unbelievably pleased. Closing my eyes, I continue to work him, my nerves coming alive. My pussy screams to take this massive man inside of me.

"Can I touch your breasts?"

My eyes open. His gaze is locked on my chest. "You can touch anything you want."

He reaches up and cups each of my breasts. I hold myself still, watching him, wondering what he'll do. His fingers run along the sensitive skin of my chest, then slide across my nipples. I gasp in pleasure, and he moves back to my nipples, rubbing them again.

I moan, and he looks completely fascinated as he rubs them harder and harder, and then pinches them. Unable to help myself, I begin to rub myself against his length once more.

He leans up after a moment and takes one of my nipples into his mouth. I cry out, and completely lose myself to this man, who seems to be obsessed with my breasts. He tastes each nipple. He sucks both deeply, grasping them as he does so. And I can't seem to think as he lavishes them with attention.

When I know that I'm going to lose my mind if I don't

have him soon, I lift up from him and grasp his dick before lowering the head of his cock into my channel.

He groans beneath me, and holds my gaze as I lower myself inch by inch down on him, wincing as my body holds him too tightly at times. If I wasn't dripping, soaking wet, I don't think for a second I could fit him. But still, the fit is tight. Deliciously tight.

When I hit his hilt, I grab one of his hands and push it between us, showing him how to stroke my clit. It only takes him a moment for him to get it, and then I'm wild with need. This man's hands were built for pleasure, they touch me in all the right ways, and his lips return to lavishing my breasts.

When I start to ride him, taking him in and out of my tight channel, we both begin to swear. The pleasure…it's unimaginable. So good that all thoughts have left my mind. So good that the world outside of our bodies fades to nothing.

We fuck harder and harder until he's forced to stop sucking on my breasts, because I'm riding him so damn hard. His name slips from my lips as he pinches my clit, and then I go wild. Now his name isn't a moan, it's a scream of pleasure, a prayer, and when he comes, I orgasm, exploding over the edge, riding him as our slick bodies smack together over and over again until I collapse on top of him.

I'm pretty sure sex has never been this good before.

Hell, I *know* sex has never been this good before.

This Adam has filled my "sex pot" so full that I don't think I'll ever need to be fucked again. And yet, I feel him harden inside of me.

"I can touch you anyway I want?" he asks softly, running his lips against my hair.

I nod, still spinning with pleasure.

He rolls on top of me, and before I have a chance to say a word again, we're fucking once more.

Hell, was I worried he'd only have the energy for one round? Now I was pretty damned sure I'd be his fuck-toy all day long.

And I was finding it hard not to love that idea…

Chapter Thirteen

EMORY

Where was she? Where was Kiera? And why the hell was she down here in the first place?

And did she hear it all? Did she know the truth about me?

My mind spins as I race through the fucking tunnels beneath the school. When Mario and his friends had grabbed me, I'd thought this day couldn't get any worse. Not only was I in a reform school, where not "reforming" was a death sentence, but I wasn't even out of my brother's grasp. Something that I thought would be the only benefit of the damned place.

I guess I was wrong on that account too.

I'd told Mario whatever the fuck I had to say to get out of his underground lair. *Things I would never want Kiera to hear.* Later, I could pick off Mario and his crew one at a time, freeing myself from my brother's grasp and making my time at the reform school at least bearable. Then I'd have nothing to worry about except surviving each day.

Unless I got out at the end of my sentence.

But I couldn't bring it in me to care about what would happen if I ever got out. All I cared about was protecting

Kiera. I needed to keep her out of my brother's grasp, no matter what it cost me.

And then I'd spotted Kiera in the tunnels.

For one terrible moment, I'd wondered what the hell I was supposed to do. The second they found out who she was, they'd have the numbers to drag her off to my brother. But if they didn't know who she was, she'd be killed as a spy.

It'd seemed like a no-win situation. All I'd known is that I had to reach her first, and do whatever the hell I had to in order to protect her.

Except then she'd gone and disappeared.

"Fuck," I mutter, stopping for the first time since seeing her.

I was pretty damned sure I'd searched all the tunnels down here, and I could hear Mario and his men scrambling through the tunnels too. But the fact that they were still searching too meant none of us had found her. And the only way that was possible was if she'd gone back to the surface, or found a place none of us could reach.

Breathing hard, I look up and spot a grate, the ladder in the wall just barely visible. If Kiera disappeared, I had to assume she knew the tunnels beneath the school better than we did…somehow. And if she did, she was bound to leave.

Eventually.

So I release a panicked breath, and I start up the stairs. Beneath my skin, I can feel my other side rolling. There and ready to be let free, should I need it. I practice deep breaths until the feeling eases. Going berserk right now is the last thing I need.

Pushing open the grate, I climb out.

Leaning against the wall is a man I recognize, one of my brother's men from a lifetime ago. A guy my brother had sent here as a young boy. My jaw drops. *He sure as hell has gotten bigger, but he's got the same red hair and dark freckles.*

"Jasper?"

He doesn't smile. "Emory."

We stare at each other, tension crawling between us. He and I had never been enemies before. We'd simply been two boys being tortured by a psychopath. My brother would trip him, pin him onto the ground, and pee on him. He killed his pet mouse and made him eat it while he cried.

With me…his punishments were no less twisted, but some of them were different. Two berserkers had once tried to escape his lands. Both children. He'd told me I could choose who would live or die, and if I couldn't, he'd kill them both. He told me he was teaching me why I should be grateful to never be our people's leader.

Instead he taught me how to hate.

"I didn't know where you ended up when you left."

His hazel eyes narrow. "I'm not surprised. You never seemed to know what was going on."

I shrug. I knew more than I led on.

"Or maybe you didn't want to know."

"Maybe," I say quietly.

More silence.

"So, you leaving the tunnels? That means you're either a mutant lover or one of Mario's men."

"Mutants?" I tense, imagining the crazed beasts finding Kiera alone.

He smirks. "If you didn't know about the mutants, then you must have been there for Mario."

"I wasn't given much of a choice," I say.

But I don't say more. I don't know where Jasper's loyalties lie, and if anyone suspects that I'm not loyal to my brother, my life is over. Inside the reform school or out of it, it didn't matter.

"You didn't enjoy spending time with your brother's lackeys?" he asks, his face expressionless.

"Do you?" I ask instead of answering.

He stands up straighter. "Be careful, Emory. A lot of people around here hate Maxen. They might not exactly appreciate his bastard brother being here."

"Good to know," I grate out.

He starts to walk away, then pauses. "Did he turn you into the man he wanted?"

Something in my chest twists. "I hope not."

He gives a sharp nod. "Good," he says, and leaves.

I stare after him for a while, then position myself far enough away from the grate to be able to watch for Kiera. Hours pass. I see Mario and his men leave, but no Kiera. The sun begins to set. Still nothing.

A horrible feeling washes over me. *What if she's been back in her dorm room all along?* What if his men found her there instead?

I decide the hell with it and head back toward the berserker house a guard had pointed out to me. But along the way I run into a group of berserkers being led by a huge man.

"Dinner time," one of them says. "And we get to eat with the others today. How nice."

"But my friend—"

"The berserker house is empty. Go eat."

Could she already be at the cafeteria?

I fall in line with the others, but instantly notice Kiera isn't among them, or with any of the other supernaturals all drifting toward the cafeteria. *Maybe she's in the cafeteria already?*

My gaze runs over a couple of mermaids, two women

with bright pink hair. One of them laughs, and I drag my gaze away from them. Kiera should be somewhere safe, laughing with her friends.

If only I'd stayed far away from her.

My stomach twists. *She could be anywhere in this damned place.*

We enter two doors that are thrown wide and fall in line, entering a huge cafeteria room. Each of us is given a tray and decent-looking food is set out, some kind of stew, mashed potatoes, and jello. I walk through the line, barely aware of what I'm doing, my gaze searching for her in the crowd.

"Keep going," someone snarls behind me.

I startle when I realize I've reached the end of the line.

What do I do now? Go back to the tunnels? Search her dorm room? Or wait and see if she arrives?

I turn and spot Mario and the other berserkers. I feel a huge rush of relief to know she's at least safe from them. But I also decide to stay as far from the bastards as I can. The last thing I want is people associating me with Mario and his crew, or getting a knife in the back for being Maxen's brother.

I sit down at a table with one other big man, but completely ignore him, searching for any sign of Kiera. But she's still nowhere to be found.

"You're a berserker, right?" the man across from me asks, and the arrogance in his voice makes me think he's a fae for the briefest moment before I remember just how big he is.

Definitely not a fae.

I finally look at him. He sits in the center of his side of the table, a giant of a man who holds himself like a damned king. He's got the polished look of an aristocrat, with light brown hair neatly styled and one of those pretty-boy faces. I glance at his muscular arms and realize that he doesn't wear the branding of a berserker. *So what is he? Definitely not a vamp, a phoenix, or a Nephilim.*

That left a shifter. A *very* big shifter.

"Who's asking?" I say, studying him.

He huffs, and I swear there's a little smoke when he does so. "Drake, you insolent little prick."

I reach for my fork and start eating. *Insolent little prick?* Well, maybe I don't have any answers for the asshole.

"You know all the berserkers?" he presses.

I keep eating and ignore him.

He leans forward, crowding my space. "You know a female berserker with long, white-blonde hair and big boobs?"

I swear the food in my mouth turns to ash. *Did he seriously just ask me about my Kiera? Did he really talk about her boobs?* "Watch it, asshole."

"You know her!" he says, triumph in his voice. "Where is she?"

"I wouldn't tell you if you were the last god damn goat shifter on the planet."

"I'm no goat," he growls. "You, berserker, have met a dragon. You, berserker, better change your tone before you're nothing but burned meat."

A dragon? It takes everything in me not to look at him again. I've never met a dragon shifter. The shifters were like kings of the sky and the earth… far more powerful than the rest of us. If it wasn't for the fact that they typically only had one child, it would've been impossible to hunt them to the point of near extinction. In another time and another place, I'd have a million questions for him.

But not when he was asking about Kiera.

I smirk at him, hiding the awe that creeps up inside of me. I'm used to fucking bullies, even a damned dragon wasn't going to intimidate me. "If you think I'm telling you a thing about Kiera, you better go clean your scales, or count your treasure, whatever you lizards like to do."

Instead of reacting, he smiles. "You know her name. You're defensive. You *know* her."

I hate that he figured that out. I glare, digging into the mashed potatoes that have an unpleasant watery texture.

"I want to know more about her."

"I'm sure you do," I mutter.

"Life can be easy for you, berserker, or hard. The way you answer my questions can help determine that."

I lift my gaze to meet his. "Why do you want to know anything about her? You think you're the first guy to see her and want to bang her?"

"It's not that," he says.

I glare. "Then what is it?"

He leans in closer and lowers his voice. "I'm pretty sure the female is my mate."

Chapter Fourteen

KIERA

I stroke Adam's chest, glad that the light from the crystals growing from all over the cave might not be enough for him to see me blushing. After our fifth round, the big man seemed to finally calm. He'd gathered me close, and covered me with his oddly soft, woven blanket. At first he'd held me so tightly it felt like he'd been afraid I'd run away, but slowly his grip had loosened until things just felt…comfortable between us.

Which was about the time I'd started thinking about everything that had happened.

I still didn't understand it. One minute I'd been whirling, realizing that the stranger who saved me was my childhood friend, and one of Lord Maxen's lackeys, and the next I'd been in the arms of this man. I've never felt attraction like this in my life. Like it overpowered all logic.

Even now the attraction was still there, although calmer now that I was satisfied. I was finally able to think clearly. *What had I done?* I'd slept with this Adam. This Adam who was a virgin, who seemed to have lived a horrible life. I needed to go back to reality and face my new life at this reform school, and Maxen's allies, but how could I just leave this man?

I had no idea.

"Why were you sent here?" Adam asks, his deep voice rolling through me.

I shiver, not wanting to think of Lucy and the vampires. "I killed some men."

He doesn't react. "Oh."

"Why were you sent here?" I ask, trying to imagine what could be so bad that hearing about me killing a bunch of people didn't even make him flinch.

"I killed the scientists that made me. At first the Enforcers said that I wasn't human, that I should be destroyed, but a man argued that I was a living being, one capable of understanding what I'd done. They chose this reform school rather than death, which is the fate of the others of my kind. It was lucky."

It's hard to keep my mouth shut when I want to tell him that doesn't sound lucky at all. If a berserker was tortured and tested on, and we killed our captors, there wouldn't be a trial. There wouldn't be anything. They would say our captors got what they deserved.

But mutants have never been seen as our equals.

"I'm glad you killed them," I say.

This time he does stiffen. "Why?"

My gaze moves up to his. "Creating lives just as test subjects is wrong in all kinds of ways." When he looks confused, I add, "Hasn't anyone ever told you that before?"

He's quiet for a minute. "There was a cat…"

"A cat?"

He nods. "They brought a cat in…one they stole off the street and tested on. They never noticed anything special about him, but I did. After a while, he could talk to me…in my head. He told me everything they did to us was all wrong." He strokes my hair. "When I killed them and broke us out, it was for him, for Princess. He wanted to get back to his girl. The girl who he'd lived with every day before they took him. I had nowhere to go, so I just waited until the Enforcers came."

I don't cry easily, but hell, it takes me a long minute to push down my tears. "That was…nice of you."

His hand stills. "I just wish he found his girl."

I look up at him, at the sadness in those startling gold eyes of his. "He didn't?"

I swear tears reflect in his eyes before he blinks them away. "He tracked me down here. The girl was gone when he got back. Not moved. Something about cancer."

Oh, hell. "I'm so sorry."

"I am too. Even though I like having Princess here."

I'm too sad to even comment about him having a male cat named Princess. "At least you're the proud owner of a cat."

He looks startled. "I don't own him. He's my friend."

I smile and kiss his lips lightly. *God damn, this Adam is too sweet for his own good.*

"He does what he wants, but I'm going to introduce him to you the next time he's around."

"I'd like that," I say, and then I sigh and sit up.

He sits up with fast movements. "What are you doing?"

I comb my fingers through my wild hair, trying to tame it. "I probably need to go back."

He shakes his head. "No, you don't, Kiera. The men you saw are bad men. They're going to want to hurt you."

"I don't care," I say. "It's reform or die, right? I can't even imagine what will happen to me for missing my classes today, but I'm going to take the punishment and deal with it. Because I need to get out of here. I need to graduate and get back to my family."

"Kiera," he says my name very slowly. "I've never seen a berserker graduate."

I stiffen. "What are you talking about?"

He touches my face gently. "A lot of the houses actually have graduations that end in them leaving, but I've never seen a berserker graduate. They push you until you lose control and then they use that as an excuse to say you're too dangerous to leave."

My stomach turns. "Well, I'm not going to give them any excuses."

I don't say that I probably have less control over that side of myself than the other berserkers because it's new to me. I don't say that I'm not even sure what I'd do if someone pushed me, because none of it matters, I'm going to get home.

"Getting out of here is important to you," he says, very slowly.

I nod. "My parents, my brothers, my friends, they're going to be missing me."

He kisses me lightly the way I kissed him. "Then I'll help you get out."

"You could come too," I say.

He doesn't meet my eyes. "Maybe."

"My people don't care about mutants." They did, but not like most other people. If I brought Adam to our town, my father would accept him, as long as he never showed himself to be a danger to our people.

"Maybe," he says again.

We dress slowly. Then Adam leads me out of his little cave a different way than we came in. We end up climbing a ladder and pushing a grate up. Outside, we're at the edge of the woods.

There, he pauses and strokes his hand down my arm. "I am technically part of the house of Almost Humans, but no one cares what I do. I spend most of my time in the tunnels, or the forest. But for you, I'll try."

"Try?" I ask, confused.

"Try to 'reform.'"

I smile. "You do that, because you're coming with me when I leave this hell hole."

He smiles back, a shy smile.

And then I think of something, and my pleasure fades away. "We should be careful…about the way people perceive our relationship. There are some…complications, and I don't want to bring you down with me if there's trouble."

His gaze leaves mine. "It's okay, Kiera. I didn't expect you to tell others about me."

My heart twists. "That's not what I—"

"We should go to your house, before it's too late." He starts to walk back toward my new home, and I hurry after him, trying to figure out what the hell to say to make things better between us.

"I'm not embarrassed about you," I tell him.

"We should hurry," he says over his shoulder.

Somehow, the reform school feels a little colder.

Chapter Fifteen

DRAKE

Anger rolls through me as I emerge from the shower, dry, and toss on my clothes. Kiera, the berserker, was not in any of my other classes. She was not in the dining hall. And the tall berserker, the one I now know is named Emory, wouldn't tell me anything more.

It was as if she had just disappeared.

Which was annoying as hell.

Two women had come to my door during the night. Both of them I'd sent away. I didn't need just any woman riding my cock, I needed the blonde-haired berserker.

Did she know that she'd been driving me wild since our first meeting? Did she suspect that she might be my mate? Or was all of this just a game to her?

I didn't know, but I was going to find out. *This* morning.

On the bottom floor of the shifter house is a smaller dining room and a kitchen. There's always food here, because shifters are always hungry. I go to the table and fill a plate with ham, eggs, and bacon. I tear into the food, then wash it all down with milk.

Hunger sated, I ignore the other shifters who scatter out of the way of a bigger predator and head for our training class. I tell myself it's just so I can see her early, but a nagging voice in the back of my mind remembers the students who have died in this class. Our teacher never stops things when they get bad. Our teacher smiles when the life drains from our eyes.

And Kiera…she had pissed him off.

My dick rises at the memory, and I scold my dragon. The damn beast inside of me loves a feisty woman, a woman who challenges him, but this is not the place for a female like that. She should shut her mouth and survive here.

Even though I doubt she could.

It's an easy walk from the shifter house to the training ground outside of the berserker house. Just past the House of Phoenixes. Our houses are toward the back of the reform school, giving us a small forest for the shifters to race through, and ending in a jagged cliff near the ocean. If they hadn't destroyed my wings, this would be the kind of place my dragon would soar over, claiming everything beneath him as our own.

My heart twists at the thought, and the stirring of the air around me reminds me briefly of the feel of flying. But not really. Just a poor man's pathetic need to live again.

I'm the first one to reach the training grounds, and I circle the large dirt area with irritation. Where is everyone? Where is *she*? Something in me starts to come undone. Something so powerful that I find it hard to breathe.

And then I hear a group of students approach. I whirl around and watch the berserkers with narrowed eyes. My Kiera is not among them. It's the same group of males I've seen time and time again. Men I care nothing for.

I ignore them. Half a dozen shifters join us. Our

people mingle, a strange truce between us until the fighting begins. And yet, still, no Kiera.

My dragon rages within me, and I know soon I might shift. I might turn into the powerful beast that everyone fears so much and prove to the school that I'm too dangerous to continue being here.

But I'm starting not to care.

I fight my instincts. I take deep breaths. And yet, it builds and builds. And then I spot the berserker named Emory. I march up to the damn asshole and grab him by the shirt. "Where the fuck is she?" I hiss.

For the first time, I notice that his eyes are as wild as mine. His body seems to swell before me, and I watch him more carefully when I realize that he seems to be barely holding onto his control too.

"I don't know," he growls, and his body seems to swell again.

I freeze, realization dawning on me. "You feel...something for her."

He stiffens, but doesn't answer. But he doesn't need to. I can read it in his face.

I release him. Uncertainty fills me. The female hadn't told me whether she was taken. *What the hell would I do if this man was hers? Would I kill him and claim her as my own?* No, she wasn't a shifter. That was not the berserker way. She would choose me on her own or not at all. The mate bond meant nothing to her.

I might...I might have to win this woman.

Oh, hell, this isn't going to be as easy as I thought.

The berserker suddenly looks behind my shoulder, and his expression changes. I whirl around and spot Kiera approaching the training yard. Every muscle in my body stiffens. She looks...amazing. Her hair has been swept up, tied somehow in a messy bun on her head. Little white-blonde hairs have escaped, trailing about her face, dusting her shoulders. Her almost bare shoulders. The clothes she wears are no better than the ones from yesterday.

She looks like some kind of badass. Her dark shirt is ripped on the edges and around the top in a way that's almost on purpose. Her long black leather pants are stuffed into leather boots, and she has some kind of leather and fur belt that hangs low on her hips.

It should look ridiculous, and yet, it doesn't. It simply… suits her. *There's never been a woman as beautiful as her.* The thought enters my mind, and I hate that I believe it.

I approach, and don't realize the berserker is at my shoulder until her gaze slides from him to me.

"Need something?" she asks, and there's an edge to her words.

"We have unfinished business," I say.

"So do we," the man beside me adds.

She fucking scowls at both of us. "I have nothing more that I need from *either* of you."

Then she walks the hell away from us to stand near the others. My female…walks away.

A growl slips from my lips, and I whirl to track her with my eyes. If she were a shifter, I'd simply toss her over my shoulder and take her somewhere I could prove my dominance, while she in turn did her best to dominate me. But she was not a shifter, and I had no desire to ruin things further between us, so I curl my hands into fists and refrain from touching her.

But this is far from over, I promise both her and myself.

I needed to seduce her. *But how?*

Our instructor, a demon with a hard-on for blood, comes before I can address my woman further, and I have to bite back my rage as he explains that today is a special day. I've seen these "special" days already. They've never mattered today, but with Kiera here, they've suddenly changed.

They seem too dangerous.

"Kiera," the instructor calls, and every muscle in my body tenses.

She steps away from the others, her head held high like the queen she is. Her gaze never falters as she looks at our teacher. *Like a dragon lady.* My heart glows with the thought.

"You're up first," he says.

I'm breathing hard. I won't allow this. Female berserkers lack the ability to change like the males. She has no shot against any of these warriors.

And I don't care what it costs me, I'll keep her safe.

"Chad," Mr. James calls.

I see red. Chad is the biggest fucking berserker of them all. I've watched him tear the heads off of two shifters that outweighed him. He was vicious on the best day, and a monster in his other form.

"Drake," he calls my name, surprising me.

I move away from the others and toward her, grateful that the teacher is allowing me to fight at her side. Now I won't have to 'break the rules' and jump into a fight I wasn't asked to be in. Chad was dangerous, but no one was more dangerous than I was. But when I move to stand at her side, Mr. James makes a sound of annoyance.

"No, it'll be you and Chad versus the girl."

"That's not a fight," slips from my lips. "It's a slaughter."

"We'll see," the instructor says, with that demonic little smile of his.

My hands curl until my knuckles crack. If he thinks I'm going to hurt her, he has another thing coming. Demon, teacher, I didn't give a damn, if he made me, I'd kill him. I'd killed before...

Mr. James circles behind her, and I'm shocked when he jams the needle into the back of her neck.

"Shit!" she shouts, but he's already yanked it free.

I'm surprised when Emory is suddenly at my side. "What the fuck was that?"

His anger matches my own.

Mr. James smiles. "It's not your turn yet, Emory."

The berserker opens his mouth to argue, and the instructor lifts a hand. Emory goes flying, smacks the trunk of a tree with a sickening crack, and slides down the tree. He doesn't move, and I don't blame him. The fucker probably has a broken spine.

Mr. James stabs Chad with a needle next, but he doesn't react. This isn't his first rodeo, after all.

"I feel weird," Kiera says.

I look between her and the instructor, afraid that if I argue with him again, he'll simply replace me with another shifter.

"What was that?" Her skin ripples.

I stiffen, heart pounding. "It makes berserkers lose control."

Those stunning blue eyes of hers meet mine, fear in their depths.

"It won't do anything to you," I say, but my words come out unsure.

Her skin ripples again, and I'm shocked when she makes a strange sound. Suddenly, her body begins to grow and expand. She doubles, triples, quadruples her size and keeps going. Beside me, Chad is changing too.

It's like my brain stops working. I thought I would turn on Chad and protect her. I thought the shot would do nothing to a female. Not that another female berserker had been in the reform school before…

Beside me, Chad roars.

Kiera expands her stance. She looks like herself, except like a monstrous version of herself. When Chad launches at her, she attacks right back. They roll together, using their powerful bodies against each other.

I hear gasps around me.

My brain begins to work again.

Leaping into the flurry of movement, I manage to shove Chad back from her. He snarls at me, but then it's her fist that connects with the side of my face. I hiss in pain, surprised that the female could hurt me in any form, and surprised that the woman I'm protecting injured me.

"I'm on your side," I growl.

But either she doesn't understand, or she doesn't care. She launches herself at me, but Chad meets her halfway there. They begin to tumble together again. Punching, kicking, losing control.

Seeing my female hurt, being attacked by another male, changes something inside of me. I don't care that she's changed forms. I don't care that she hit me. I just want her safe.

My fist connects with the side of his head, and his gaze jerks to me. When he leaps off of her and onto me, I'm prepared. Berserkers are stronger than shifters in this form, but they aren't as fast, they aren't as agile. I land a kick to his gut, then spring out of the way before his larger body can cover mine. We circle each other, his giant fists coming at me over and over again, like he's a man made of stone, but only one manages to land, and I clamp down on the grunt of pain that slips from my lips.

When I hear Kiera make a sound, my gaze snaps to her, not sure if I should be prepared for her to come after me again, or if something's wrong. The slight distraction was a mistake. Chad's fist hits the side of my head, and I tumble to the ground. Before I can leap free, he's on me, his massive body crushing the air from my lungs. His fists begin to pummel the sides of my head, and for the first time in my life, fear uncurls inside of me.

I reach for my dragon form, even knowing that shifting into my inner beast will seal my fate here…and that the others will see the horror of what was done to me. That the others will see that I'm not a true dragon anymore.

Kiera is suddenly standing behind Chad. She slams him in the nose with her palm, and when he releases me, she smashes him two more times in the head. The giant slides off of me and hits the ground. His eyes go dull, and then his muscles go limp. Slowly, his body begins to shrink and returns to normal.

I half-expect Kiera to do the same. I half-expect her to come after me again.

Instead, she turns toward Mr. James.

I don't know what she has planned when she picks up the demon and chucks him. He hits the trunk of a tree near Emory and slides to the ground, unmoving. Then the massive Kiera stalks through the crowd as everyone shrinks back. She kneels down beside Emory and touches his face gently. Slowly, oh so slowly, her body grows smaller, and she returns to normal.

She's dirty. Bruised. Bleeding from several places. One side of her face is swollen. But she leans over Emory, touching his face.

His eyes open, unfocused at first.

I rise to my feet, even though my head pounds and my face feels bruised and swollen. I drag myself toward them, watching the two, my heart in my throat. Emory isn't the only one that just took a hell of a beating. Hell, the berserker didn't last against a fucking demon. So why was she checking on him?

"Kiera?" he says, sounding confused.

"Are you okay?" she asks.

He nods, then slowly struggles to his feet.

"Anything broken?"

"No, but—"

"Good," she says, and then she clocks him.

I don't know if she's damn good with her hands, if he wasn't ready for it, or if he's just weak, but he falls back over. Then she spins around on her heel. When she spots me, her eyes narrow, and I'm a little thankful when she walks on by.

Over her shoulder, she calls, "Class dismissed."

A guy beside me says, "*Dammmn.*"

A female shifter chuckles. "That was awesome."

"Uh, I'm not sure Mr. James is still alive."

I turn and spot a shifter male leaning over our teacher, his hand feeling for a pulse. A pit in my stomach forms. If Kiera killed a teacher, it didn't matter the circumstances, she was done for.

"We have to protect her."

I jerk and realize Emory has come to stand beside me. Normally, I'd find the berserker addressing me annoying. But for once, I thought I might just need an ally…if I was going to keep Kiera alive.

"You got a plan?"

Chapter Sixteen

KIERA

The Dean of Discipline glares at me over his desk. His fingers are steepled in front of his mouth, his tie askew and sweat beading his shaved head. "Explain it to me again. Explain why your teacher is in our medical ward, having sustained massive injuries from something you did to him."

I try to keep my voice light. "Again, I'm not really sure—"

"I have a dozen students that saw you go berserk."

My mouth closes. *Should I keep denying it?*

He sighs and leans back in his chair. "And yet, a female who can go berserk…that's unbelievably rare. I did some research. Are you aware that only two women have had that ability, as far as our history books are concerned?"

I'd known it was rare. I hadn't known it was *that* rare.

"The House of Berserkers still wants you, Kiera. If you decide to become the wife of the king, we can arrange your departure—"

"No." I didn't know a lot of things, but I knew I wasn't going to become that monster's bride.

"Kiera—"

"Would you want your daughter to marry him?" I ask, the question a snap of anger.

He flinches and avoids my gaze. "If you remain here, there will be consequences for what you've done. Consequences I'm not sure you'll survive from."

"Would you choose it over marrying that fucking asshole?"

He sighs again, louder than before, and finally looks at me again. "In the Wicked Reform School, the line between right and wrong is paper thin…and it moves a bit. I do a lot of things I'm not proud of, but I'm not in the business of selling women. If you decide not to go to the king, I won't protect you here, but I also won't make you go."

My hands unclench, and I wipe my sweaty palms on my knees. "Good. I won't go."

"You'll take the punishment?"

I don't like the sound of that, but I nod.

He lifts up his phone and pushes a button. After a minute, he speaks. "Go ahead and arrange the punishment for injuring a teacher."

When he sets the phone down, he motions for me to leave the office.

I rise, but stop at the door. "Dean?"

"Yes?"

"Do berserkers ever…serve their time? Do they ever get out?"

He's quiet for a long time before saying, "I have things to do."

What he doesn't say lays heavy on me as I close the door.

I leave his office. Outside, the secretary looks worried. "Henry will show you where to go."

My stomach sinks as the silent golem leads me across

the campus. I honestly can't believe this is only my second day, and I've already managed to screw up so badly. It wasn't that I blamed myself for what happened. Mr. James forced me to change. It was just that my plan to obey the rules and get out of here was looking more and more like a pipe dream.

That was if I could even survive until "graduation."

The afternoon sun beats down at us as we pass the dining hall. I take a deep breath, inhaling the scents of meat and potatoes. Despite my resolve to endure this punishment without showing weakness, my stomach grumbles. Berserkers ate. A lot. And since coming to the reform school, I'd missed far too many meals already.

We walk through a lonely field and reach three buildings near the edge of the woods that surround the school. A sad sign says "detention center" in front of them. The silent golem leads me to the first building, produces a key from his pocket, and unlocks the door.

I take a deep breath. *So, isolation was the punishment?* Isolation I could handle.

"Enter," the golem orders.

I start forward, into the darkness.

Behind me, the golem starts to close the door. "I'll return, for your body."

I whirl around to ask him more, but the door clicks shut and locks behind me. *Well, that's not good.* I turn back to the pitch black of the room and start forward. My front foot comes down too far, and I'm almost sent flying, but manage to pull back in time.

Heart racing, I sit down and scoot forward. This time, I feel the stairs. I move slowly down the tight, winding steps, even though I have no idea what the hell waits for me deep in the ground.

Time ticks forward and I know I've been scooting

forward for too long. A sudden panic fills me, and I wonder if I'm going to be trapped in darkness forever. If this was really their plan, for me to get lost in this place and starve to death. I debate going back the way I came, but then grit my teeth and force myself to keep going.

If I let them get in my head, I'll go crazy.

Time passes slowly, and my movements become a pattern. Scoot forward, feel for the next step, move down, over and over again. I'm about to scream when I realize that light is bleeding into the darkness. Moving faster, I finally come around the twisting stairs and spot a room, a few flickering lights illuminating the space.

Wincing against the light, I stand and step out into the room.

My jaw drops open. In every direction, bodies of creatures litter the room. Blood paints the floor and the walls. I move slowly around the giant walls of yellow stone and circle the pillars. My breathing hitches as I hear the sound of water flowing on one side of the room and spot a bed in the center of the room.

Drawing closer, I realize someone is in the bed, lying down. A man.

But who?

Probably the man who killed all these creatures.

My heart lurches, and my hands curl into fists as I ready myself for a fight.

Suddenly, my boots scuff the floor, and I feel the air in the room change. The man in the bed slowly sits up, and I'm shocked when I spot the big shifter, Drake.

He grins at me. "Took you long enough."

"Wh—what are you doing here?"

He shrugs. "I knew they'd bring you here, so I took care of the flesh eaters for you."

My jaw drops. "Why?"

He stretches and my gaze slides down his bare, muscular chest and lingers on the thin sheet that covers him. *Is he wearing clothes?* My blood heats up. *What if he isn't?*

"I didn't want anything bad to happen to you."

"Because you enjoy a woman who can kick your ass?" slips from my lips before I realize that reminding the big shifter of what I'd done might not be the best thing to do.

"No," he says, drawing out the word. "Because...I'm pretty damned sure you're my mate."

His...mate? Now I know my jaw is hanging open again. "Not a chance."

He either doesn't hear me or pretends not to. "Does that berserker complicate things?"

"Beserker?"

"Emory."

I stiffen at his name. "Why would he complicate anything?"

"He isn't your male?"

"No!"

He smiles. "Good."

My thoughts move to Adam. "But that doesn't mean I don't have...someone."

His smile turns dangerous. "Who is he?"

"None of your business."

"If another male claims you as his own, then it's my business."

"I didn't say he claimed me as his own," I say, rolling my eyes. "No one claims me as their own."

He rises from the bed, and I see he's wearing nothing but dark boxers. And that he's hard as fuck.

Something inside of me awakens. This shifter is an arrogant asshole. He's also big and sexy. Different from the berserkers back home. He holds himself like a king, not like some crazed brute, and there's something oddly appealing about that.

"Good," he says when he comes to stand far too close to me.

I take a step back. "I didn't need you to kill these beasts for me. Or to defend me in fighting class."

His gaze holds mine. "I protect what's mine."

"I'm not anyone's."

He runs a hand slowly down my arm, and I hate that I shiver. "Why fight this, Kiera?"

I hold his gaze. "I don't think you get it. Just a few days ago I was just a normal berserker. I lived with my family, my parents and brothers, and I'd just graduated. I had friends," I swallow down the wave of pain that comes with the thought of Lucy, "and a life."

"We were all like that before the reform school, but life goes on."

My jaw clenches so hard it hurts. "Yeah, it does. But I'm no more going to become your mate than I'm going to become the wife of Lord Maxen. My goal is to finish my time here and go back to my old life."

His gaze grows calculating. "Who is Lord Maxen?"

Is that the part he focused on? "Lord Maxen is a giant asshole who runs the House of Berserkers and thinks he's our king. And, I guess, because of some prophecy about a female who can go berserk, he's decided that I'm going to become his wife."

I swear every muscle in his body tightens. "Well, that's not going to happen."

"No, it's not, and I'm also not going to be your mate, so get over it."

He lets out a loud sigh, like I'm a really irritating child. "Seduction then…"

"What?"

He draws even closer, and I have to fight the urge to take another step back. "You should know that a mate bond is nearly impossible to resist. This thing between us is going to happen. It's just a matter of when."

My brain has stopped working, and I can't stop my gaze from sliding from his ridiculously handsome face, down his chest, and to that hard erection of his. I want to argue against Drake. He's so damned arrogant and cocky that I want to resist him just to resist him, but greeting me half-naked makes it fucking hard.

When he pulls back from me, I'm surprised by the wave of regret that moves through me. But then he plunks himself down on the bed, lying back in the most casual way, his erection still hard and straining. "So, if you don't want to have sex, how do you want to spend our next few days here?"

"You're going to stay here with me?" I ask, and my words come out too high.

He grins. "You bet. It was hard enough to get in here… and, of course, magic the bed. I don't even want to tell you the deal I had to make with the witches… so I can't exactly just climb right back out, not without the key."

I stare at him, then back at the area covered in dead flesh eaters and a dark, twisting staircase.

I might be better off there.

Chapter Seventeen

KING MAXEN

My other form slowly shrinks away as I pant, trying to calm myself. Around the sides of the cell, the chained berserkers are no more than hanging pieces of flesh. The sounds of their screams and pleas still fill my ears.

Smiling, a shudder moves through my body, and I feel my cock grow hard. In my mind, I can picture the moment they realized the injection I'd given them kept them from shifting. That they were helpless.

Their faces were a mask of terror. Pure and utter terror.

Another shudder of pleasure racks my body, and I stand in the middle of it all, drinking in this perfect moment when my senses are sharpest. When I feel most alive.

"Your Majesty?"

I turn and reach for the towel before Bill throws it to me, then carefully mop the blood and chunks of flesh from my body. "Do you have news of my queen?"

Already, I'd set to work on House of Berserkers. *Everything must be as perfect as my new bride when she arrives.*

"There have been...some delays."

"Delays?" Something dark rumbles inside of me.

Bill takes a nervous step back. "The dean has taken your bribes to communicate with the female about the possibility of being your bride. Unfortunately, it seems from his messages, she's...reluctant to leave the reform school."

"Reluctant to leave?" The question comes out ice cold. "What female would refuse me?"

"Apparently," he clears his throat in that irritating way again, "the female in question is Kiera Frost, daughter to the Lord of the Winter Berserkers."

"Fuck," I mutter.

The other lords would've been smart enough to tell their children to obey me at all costs. They would have taught their sons and daughters to fall in line before me or die at my hands. But not the Lord of the Winter Berserkers, Lord Frost himself. The man was stubborn, arrogant, and an asshole that had long since served his purpose.

"I will have her, whether she agrees to the match or not."

Bill shifts from foot to foot.

"What is it?" I snap.

"I just...the prophecy says that the female must take a mate by choice. That it can't be forced, or the prophecy will not be fulfilled."

Hell, I did remember something about that whole personal freedom thing. "Well, we shall get her here, and then worry about the rest of it."

"Very good, King Wolff." He bows. "But there is more."

"What?"

"The female has been sent for discipline. Apparently, with a room full of flesh eaters."

My flesh ripples, and I feel myself expanding. "Do they not understand how precious she is?"

"Th—they do, but—"

"Have my men free her. Now. No matter the cost." I feel my vision going red. "I will have her, even if she isn't in one piece, I will have her. And if anyone should stand in my way, they will die."

Bill is halfway out the door. "Yes, Your Highness."

"Send in more prisoners!" I roar.

"Yes, Your Highness!" he says, out the door and out of sight.

I turn back to the bodies on the walls, and not caring if I use my hands, feet, or mouth, I tear their bodies into smaller pieces. *This…Kiera dared to refuse me?*

Well, I said that she would be my queen. I *didn't* say that she had to like it. And if she continued to refuse me, her life might just get very, very bad.

And if that wasn't enough…there was always her family.

I feel my massive face twist and an animalistic laugh leaves my lips as I tear an arm off a hanging body. That was the thing about caring for anything. If I'd taught Emory anything, it was that doing so was a weakness.

A weakness that I could use against people.

Luckily for me.

Chapter Eighteen

ADAM

I told myself that when the female left, when she walked away without looking back, I'd let her go. I wouldn't try to succeed at this reform school when I wasn't even sure it was what she wanted.

But something inside of me wouldn't let me let her go. Something chewed and ate at my belly until I found myself on Princess's favorite tree in a quiet part of the gardens. It was late at night, long past the time students were allowed to roam free, but I knew the guards' rotations. I knew how to avoid them.

You're troubled.

I turn and spot Princess as he leaps slowly up the branches until he reaches me. He walks like a king across my branch and moves toward me. I wait, as I always do, until he lowers his head, and then I pet him gently.

"Yes," I say, my word disturbing the silence of the night.

Why?

I feel him purr beneath my touch and rub the spot behind his ears that he likes, while I decide how to explain my troubles. "I met a female. She smelled good. She felt good. She was…different than anyone I've met before. We had sex, and then she left. I miss her. I want her. But I know what I am."

Humans, Princess huffs in my head.

"What?" I ask softly, praying that Princess will explain these things that I don't understand, the way he always does.

Why don't you deserve her? Because of what you are? He huffs again. *I have met many males in my life, of many different kinds, and you are a good one. She would be lucky to have you.*

"You don't understand. Even before I was Adam—" I stop, shocked by my words.

There was never anyone before. I have only ever been Adam. Hadn't they told me that over and over again? Hadn't the scientists told me that my memories of a mother with a sad smile were all in my head? Hadn't they told me that my dark room and mattress on the floor, with a stuffed bear with one eye, was something I'd made up?

Whoever you were before. Whoever didn't want you before. They were wrong, Adam. You were always good. Always.

I feel my eyes prickle, even though I don't understand why. Princess moves so that I'm scratching his body. "I haven't seen her since then. She's…disappeared."

When my girl disappeared, I went and looked for her. Look for your female and don't ever give up.

"You stopped looking for your girl."

He moves out of my reach again, and I know I've hurt him, I just don't know why.

I didn't give up on her. I will see her again. That I know with all my heart.

"Okay," I agree, even though I still don't understand. I just know I don't want to cause him pain.

What was your female?

"A berserker."

Then we should go to the berserker house and find her.

"But if anyone sees me…"

They will learn that even a mutant will go after what he desires.

I'm still uncertain, but I climb down the tree, following Princess's agile movements. We move through the shadows of the forest, his multicolored fur blending in with his surroundings, and we avoid the areas with dangerous creatures. Going around the outside of the thickest part of the woods, we come to the cliffs that overhang the ocean.

For a minute, I pause. Massive hippocampuses leap from the waves, the seahorses glow beneath the moon's light. They lift their horse-like heads in the air, and their bodies flash with gold and blue before they disappear back into the waters, a splash of their finned tails all that remains.

"They're beautiful," I say.

They make me hungry, Princess replies, sounding irritable.

I make a note to catch him another bird. He can do it himself, but he likes the gesture. As long as I don't pretend it's because he's my cat. He belongs to the little girl.

We circle until we come to the outside of the House of Berserkers. I've seen the white-washed building many times in the night, and never cared for the beasts inside, but now I stare hard. Is my Kiera inside?

I'll find her room. Princess sends the thought into my mind, then slinks toward the building.

I wait, feeling time ticking away. I've never felt an urge to be around the other students here. I make it a point to avoid as many of them as possible. But with the appearance of Kiera, my life seems to be changing. Even now, I'm taking a risk I never imagined.

More time passes. So much that I begin to worry. But

as I take a step out of the shadows, I spot Princess, and my racing heart slows. If anything were to happen to him…

I found her room. Something has happened. Hurry, before the guards return.

Sprinting from the trees to the buildings, I open the door to the House of Berserkers silently. Princess leads me down a hall, as if he's been here a million times before, then stops before a door. I turn the handle and find it unlocked.

Pushing open the door, I stare in surprise at her room. Clothes have been thrown everywhere. A couple of pictures are broken on the ground.

Come on, and close the door.

I do as Princess asks, and automatically open the window, so he can have an easy escape. Princess is like me. He doesn't like small cages, or places with only one exit.

Then I go slowly through her room. Her clothes. They smell like her. Like flowers and leather.

I clutch one of her shirts in my hand and kneel down. Picking a picture off the floor, I see Kiera. She looks tiny, surrounded by an older man and woman, and five big men.

Her family, Princess says.

And for once, I already knew that. They look like her, this family. The mother has white-blonde hair, cut short, but unique, just like Kiera. The father has dark hair, but the same startling blue eyes. And the brothers behind her had the same hair as their father, and his eyes.

Family. The word echoes in my mind.

My only family is Princess. But seeing these people together, I can understand why Kiera wants to leave this place. She has something to go home to.

I pick up a book and find a photo album. Settling myself against the side of her bed on the floor, I review the photos beneath the moonlight. They start with photos of a little girl who can only be Kiera. I find myself smiling as I see her messy, covered in mud. I feel a strange longing when I see her cooking with her mother, and sparring with her father and brothers.

Family. I don't know why the word hurts.

Adam? Someone was here. Someone went through her stuff.

I stiffen and look around the room. He was right. "But why?" And then it occurs to me. "The berserkers in the tunnels saw her. What if they took her? What if they hurt her?"

Then you need to find her.

My gut tightens. He's right.

"What the fuck?"

I stiffen and turn to the door. A man stands in the doorway. A huge man with a dark beard and an angry expression.

"What are you doing in Kiera's room?" he asks, a threat in his voice.

I rise slowly. "What are *you* doing in her room?"

He closes the door slowly behind him. When he turns to face me, I can see that he's come to some kind of conclusion. "Are you helping them, mutant?"

"Helping—"

He launches himself at me. I hear Princess hiss in warning, and he leaps to the windowsill as the man slams into me. But I don't have time to spring free. His huge body is suddenly on top of me, and his fists pummel my face.

Unfortunately for him, if there's one thing I know how to do, it's take a punch.

I barely feel the blows as they land, but when he leans closer, I slam my head into his nose.

He cries out, and I roll so that I'm on top of him, then

spring back. The man is easily twice my width. It doesn't matter that I'm a hair taller than him. I stand no chance in hand-to-hand combat.

Turning for the door, I start for my freedom, but his voice stops me. "If you hurt her…"

I freeze and look back at him, even though I know Princess will think I'm a fool for hesitating. "You and your kind are the ones hurting her. I'll protect her from *you*."

He's holding his nose when he looks at me, his eyes narrowed as he starts to sit up. "And who is Kiera to you?"

I don't know what I'm saying when I say it. "I think she could be my family."

His eyes widen.

"We had sex. I like her smell. And she's special to me."

He curses under his breath, but draws his hand back from his bleeding nose. "You slept with her?"

I nod. "She could be my family."

And this time when I say it, I swear my heart sings.

He sits down on the edge of her bed and wipes the blood from his nose. He looks so tired, and so alone, that something in me aches.

"Are you okay?"

"It's just…I'm working so hard to keep her safe but—" He stops talking and looks at me like he just realized who he was talking to.

"You want to keep her safe too?"

He nods, then mumbles, "Fuck it," before continuing, "I had some dragon asshole help me, and I'm pretty damn sure he screwed me over."

"How so?"

"Kiera…hurt her teacher. They sent her to the discipline—"

"No," spills from my lips, and every muscle in my body

tightens. "They have flesh eaters for the students who hurt teachers. They—"

"We tried to get in before they could, but the fucking dragon shifter used the magic to go in and I was stuck out. I came here to see if he'd gotten them both out, or if he was just going to stay with her until her sentence was over, and found you here."

My stomach twists at the idea of a dragon shifter with Kiera. "What does he want from her?"

"Probably the same thing we do."

I freeze. "You care for her too?"

"Not that she could ever feel the same way…"

I move carefully and sit down in a chair beside her small desk. "You deserve good things."

"You don't understand."

"I understand what it feels like to think you don't deserve anything good."

He looks up and our gazes hold for a long minute before he looks away. "I don't even know why I'm telling you this. I know enough to know no one can be trusted."

"I can be," I say, and mean it.

His expression is uncertain as he rises. "Now, I have the berserkers who want to hurt Kiera to kill, and a detention room to get into."

I rise too. "I'll come with you."

"No…"

"I'm going to go to her, with or without you."

He studies me for a long minute, then says, "Okay, but this doesn't mean I trust you."

"That's okay," I tell him. "I don't trust you either."

We head back out of Kiera's room, shutting the door quietly behind us. Anyone who wants to hurt Kiera will be dealt with, and then I want to see Kiera and this shifter. I need to know what all of this means.

Chapter Nineteen

KIERA

"You scared?" he asks.

I study Drake, still lounging on his bed. *Am I scared?* Maybe a little bit, but I wasn't about to tell him that.

"No," I lie, then take a deep breath and move closer to him.

He watches me with that predatory look of his, and I try to match it. All shifters think they're such badasses. Most of them are like kittens to us. Unfortunately for me, I'd never actually met a dragon shifter before. I'd actually thought they'd all been hunted to extinction.

A cat shifter, a wolf, a bear…all of them I could take. I was a little more worried about facing off with a dragon.

Still, I sit lightly at the end of his bed.

He sits up and adjusts so that his legs are crossed, then he sets his hands on his knees, palms up, and looks at me expectantly.

"What?"

"We have to touch for this to actually work."

Touch…oh, right. I'd never actually done this before. I'd

heard something about it, but that wasn't exactly the same thing.

Watching him closely, I shift on the bed, moving a little closer to him. I match the way he sits, crossing my legs and putting my hands on the tops of my knees.

"I'm doing this," I say, "but if I want to stop, we're stopping."

Drake's stunning eyes widen. "Always."

His response reassures me a little. "You do know the first time I saw you, some woman was stroking your dick."

"Jealous?" he asks, lifting a brow.

"No," I say, but my response is a little too fast. "I just thought I'd point out that you don't exactly scream 'gentleman' to me."

He flashes me a smile that's so brilliant it makes my chest ache. "Women are drawn to me. They want me. But from the moment I saw you, there was only you."

"I thought shifters liked to have a whole bunch of women."

His smile never falters. "Unless they find their mate, and then there's no one else for them."

"Berserkers aren't the same way."

His eyes narrow and his smile falters. "How so?"

"There are so few berserker women that we tend to have multiple partners. We choose more than one husband. Even my mother had two, until one of them died, long before I was born."

I swear every muscle in his body has tightened. "It wouldn't be easy for a shifter to share." I start to grin, but his words stop me. "But I can be…flexible."

"Oh?" I lift a brow.

"If this…other person is someone you can't do without."

"I told you, Emory is no one to me."

Triumph flashes in his eyes. "So there is something between you?"

I mentally let off a string of curses.

"Don't answer," he says after a long moment. "Just touch me."

I take a deep breath, rethinking this plan of mine, but then force myself to reach out and put my hands in his. His big fingers close gently around mine, and I feel a strange prickling race from his touch, and every hair on my body stands on end.

"Whoa."

"Imagine that in bed," he says, softly, but his eyes have closed.

My mind wanders to just how good he might be with his hands, and then the image is snatched away. I find myself in a dark room, sitting in front of Drake. For a second it feels like I've fallen through the damned looking glass, and then Drake's eyes meet mine.

"What do you want to know about me then?"

Oh, yes, I remember how this all started. I told him that I didn't even know him, and he'd said he had a way for us to get to know each other. I said I didn't trust him not to lie to me, and he'd suggested a way to be sure he was telling the truth.

Which had led us to Thought Sharing. Something only powerful shifters could do.

I study him and decide to start with something easy. "I want to know about your family."

His expression falters, and then he fades away. I'm suddenly standing on the balcony of a massive mansion overlooking a huge forest. A little black dragon leaps from the edge and plummets straight down. A white dragon catches him before he can hit the earth, and then two massive dragons are soaring side-by-side, the little black dragon in the grip of the white one. For a time, they release the little creature over and over again. He almost seems to catch the wind, but falls each time.

Eventually, they soar back to the balcony and land lightly near me. They shift into a beautiful woman with blonde hair, and a man as dark as she is light, with brown, closely cut hair and a teasing smile. And a little boy who looks like some strange blend of both of them and neither of them all at once.

"I want to fly!" the boy says, his little hands balling up into fists.

His dad swings him into his arms, and his voice comes out warm and gruff. "You will, son. One day."

The image fades away. The same boy, a few years older, stands in the forest. Up above, the same mansion burns. Through the trees, the bodies of a white and black dragon, tangled together, are visible, lying bleeding and broken on the blackened earth. The sounds of men's voices filter through the trees, and then the boy is running.

Tears stream down his face, and his eyes are wild. In him I can see the loss of everything. The loss of his entire world, and my heart aches.

And then, I'm sitting in front of Drake again.

For a second, I can't seem to speak. *That was him? That little boy all alone who saw his parents die?* I can't imagine what that must have been like for him. How afraid he must have been.

"Oh, Drake…"

His jaw clenches. "My family. Your turn."

Before I can say more, we blink away to my home town. I'm sitting on the porch with my mom, side-by-side on the swing. We're drinking her famous lemonade and watching the show. My five brothers and my dad roll about the yard, fighting in their human forms.

My mom and I look at each other, and then we're both laughing.

She slips her hand in mine, and we drink our lemonade and watch the sun set over the trees. Neighbors, friends pass by. And my chest squeezes.

I spent my whole life wishing I could see the world. I wanted to go to the human town. I wanted to meet other supernaturals and explore. I'd loved my home, but I'd never realized just how much until now.

And then we're back in that nothingness, just Drake and I.

"Your family seems nice."

I nod, and try to pretend tears haven't rolled down my cheeks. "They really are."

"More questions?" he asks, his gaze lingering on my tears.

"How did you end up in the reform school?"

His mouth curls into a protest, but we're whipped away.

A large black dragon is pinned to the ground. Shimmering nets pin his massive form to the ground, cutting into his scaly body. Blood leaks all over him, and there's something horrifying about seeing such an incredible creature immobilized. Men come. They surround him, knives in their hands. And I know, without having to ask, that the blades are made with dwarven steel.

My stomach lurches when they gather around him and start cutting pieces out of him, collecting them in bags as the dragon roars, but can't escape. They move to his wings, and they smirk, horrible smirks. Their blades cut into the dragon's wings over and over again, shredding the delicate substance that looks almost like massive white-gold butterfly wings.

"Put what we have in the car, then come back for the heart," one man says.

They disappear, and the dragon suddenly shifts into a man. He's injured. Horribly injured. His body shredded. But he waits in the shadows of the trees, and when the men come back, he slaughters them.

When he collapses onto the ground, he hears the sound of new voices, but he doesn't have the strength to fight. Shifting to his human form took too much energy. They stand over him, just shadows of men. They kick at his form, they mutter about the dead men, and then the image fades away.

"Drake," I whisper his name as we come back into the dark room.

Had he really been through something so terrible? Had they really destroyed his wings?

"What led *you* here?" he asks, ignoring me.

The world fades away, and I watch the events with the vampires replay. I watch my best friend die again. And when it ends, we don't come back to the dark room. We come back to the bed in the reform school. Drake gathers me in his arms, and I hate that I come undone.

Lucy should never have died that day. She should've gone on to live a long life.

All of that was taken from her.

And Drake. He should have never lost his parents just because some fucked up assholes wanted to sell his parents' bodies for parts. It was disgusting. A tragedy.

Made even worse by the fact that hunters came for him too.

None of this was fair. None of this was right. I want to fight back. I want to get angry.

But instead, I cry.

Drake says nothing, just strokes my hair, just holds me

close. For the first time since meeting him, there isn't a strange tension between us. It's just…comfortable.

When I gather myself together enough to stop crying, I whisper, "I'm tired."

The big shifter surprises me by drawing us back on the bed, wrapping me in the blanket, and settling silently under me, his hands continuing to stroke my hair.

The things I saw in his past run through my mind. I picture the boy who watched his parents die and his home burn. I watch the young man being torn apart for his pieces.

Is that the real Drake? Or is it the arrogant shifter I can't seem to escape?

My eyes close. I have no idea. But I also know that I won't be dismissing this whole mate thing quite so easily.

Being a mate to someone who wants me to get to know him seems like a hell of a lot better than being the queen to someone who wants me as his slave.

As my eyes close and sleep tugs me under, the last thought I remember is this: *but being the woman to three handsome men, that's the best.* And then, nothing else.

Chapter Twenty

EMORY

We reach the edge of the trees and stare across the field at the detention center. Outside the door, four men gather. I stare at the huge shapes for a minute before I recognize Mario and his idiots. The fact that they're outside the door that Kiera is trapped inside means they've probably figured out who the hell she is. Even for revenge they wouldn't go up against a bunch of flesh eaters.

But if my brother ordered them to, they would do anything he asked. I'd seen the fear my brother could instill in a person first-hand.

"This isn't good," I whisper to Adam.

"Us standing so close? Yes, it's awkward."

I silently curse and have to refrain from rolling my eyes. "No, not only do we need to deal with the dragon shifter, but now we have the berserkers from the tunnels to get through first."

"They've figured out she was spying on them?"

I briefly consider lying. "Probably. But I can almost

guarantee they're here to deliver Kiera to King Maxen Wolff, as he calls himself, leader of the berserkers."

"Why does he want Kiera?"

"As his bride."

Adam frowns. "She wants to marry him?"

"She's never met him."

"Then…how?"

"He wants her as his bride, so he'll have her as his bride. He doesn't really care what Kiera wants."

The mutant's expression changes. Gone is his familiar confused expression, replaced by an angry one. "No one will force her to do anything."

I'm surprised. *Doesn't he realize that one mutant means nothing to Maxen?* Adam would be no more than a body to cut down if he stood in the way of Maxen getting Kiera. Which was why we needed to kill his lackeys and buy us some time.

"We need to kill them."

"The berserkers?"

"Yes, or they'll stop at nothing to get her."

Adam frowns. "If we have to…"

"We do."

I keep myself from going berserk as we rush across the empty field. Every second that passes, I expect them to spot us, but they seem completely focused on breaking the lock to the small building. When we duck behind the third detention building, we pause, breathing hard.

Adam, I'm glad, says nothing beside me. And I take a moment to wonder why the hell I enlisted the mutant's help. Maybe because he startled me? Most mutants foamed at the mouth, couldn't put together a sentence, and were as wild as rabid wolves. To see a mutant speaking clearly and showing a soft spot for Kiera had shocked me.

But nothing had surprised me more than the revelation that they'd slept together.

I couldn't for the life of me picture Kiera with this man. Yes, over the years I'd imagined her over and over again. In every vision, she was surrounded by doting men. I wasn't sure if she'd have multiple husbands, or just spend these years having fun, but I knew that she'd be as irresistible as a woman as she had been as a girl. All the boys, myself included, would have followed her off a bridge.

And yet…she'd chosen this mutant…at least for a night.

One of the berserkers swears. I hold my breath. The second they broke the lock, we'd attack, killing two birds with one stone. But I didn't want to do it too early, or too late. This had to be perfectly timed.

After a second, I hear Mario whisper, "Almost done?"

"Almost," someone growls.

I glance at Adam. His face is an expressionless mask beneath the moonlight. For a minute, jealousy awakens inside of me. The mutant is, I begrudgingly admit to myself, handsome, but not at all like me. With his long, blond hair and startling eyes, he looks like a prince from a fantasy world.

I look like the beast out of a nightmare.

Was Adam the kind of man Kiera wanted? I push the thought aside. There could never be anything real between Kiera and I. Not as long as my brother lived. Even if she wasn't the woman he wanted, all she would ever be is someone he could hurt me through.

I wasn't here to chase the fantasy of being with her. I was here to undo the trouble I brought to her doorstep by bringing the vampires to that club. I was here to protect her from a man who would never let her go once he got her.

The ring of metal breaks through the silence of the night.

"Be careful," Mario whispers. "Whether the flesh eaters have finished her off or not, the creatures will be ready to fight."

There are some quiet sounds of acknowledgement.

I reach for the berserker side of me. Many of my kind can't control that other side of themselves at all. It simply rose up when they lost control, but couldn't be used as a tool. But for me, if I was careful, I could use the beast inside of me without becoming a slave to my blood-lust.

As long as I kept my emotions in check.

My body begins to swell, and I feel my vision growing hazy. When I reach that perfect point between beast and man, I close the connection. Then I approach our enemies. I don't know what Adam can do. I don't know if he'll be of any use at all. But it doesn't matter; with or without him, I'll destroy these men.

Mario and his men disappear inside the door of the small building, and a rumble of anger rolls through my chest. I reach the door, intending to duck down and squeeze inside. Instead, Adam leaps in ahead of me.

I hear Mario cry out. In the dark, Adam's eyes glow. Another berserker screams.

Forcing myself inside, I launch into action. Picking one man up by the legs, I bash him against the side of the building before he has time to change. Another man begins to change. I hit him in the face, hard, then leap on top of him.

Half changed, he strikes back at me, and we roll together. Suddenly, we're falling, rolling down stairs. A sound of shock twists past my lips, and I hear the berserker scream. We roll and roll, almost never-ending. There doesn't seem to be anything to grab onto.

There doesn't seem to be anything to stop us from falling for an eternity.

And then there's a light in the darkness. We hit the ground on a lower level, and I don't hesitate, even as I struggle for air. Leaping onto the berserker, I snap his neck.

I'm about to race back up the stairs to help the mutant, when I hear Kiera speak.

My thoughts swirl together. Suddenly, I'm racing through a strange half-room slick with blood and covered in pieces of flesh. I didn't want that damn dragon shifter anywhere near her, but what if he'd failed? What if Kiera was hurt by the flesh eaters?

I storm around the corner of a massive wall that separates the room in two. And freeze.

Kiera is sitting up in a bed with the dragon shifter. Her eyes are sleepy. Her hair is messy, and the dragon shifter looks naked.

"Drake!" I roar his name.

I'm swelling in size, barreling across the room before I know what I'm doing.

He's out of her arms in an instant, barely dressed, and squaring off with me. I half-expect him to shift into his other form. I expect him to do anything but stand there and wait for me to barrel him over.

But when I draw near, he slides out of my grasp and trips me in a movement almost too fast to follow. I hit the ground, the air whooshing out of my lungs. He's on me from behind, his arm around my throat, further cutting off my air.

I hear Kiera shout.

Suddenly, she's standing before me and the dragon shifter, but I can't seem to make out what she says. My ears fill with a ringing, and my vision darkens.

Death by choking. It isn't a peaceful way to go, but it beats almost anything I imagined.

And then Drake is gone.

I collapse onto the ground, sucking in shaking breaths. When I look up, Kiera is looking at me with the strangest expression. My gaze slides to a strange sound. The mutant has pinned Drake down to the ground as the big dragon shifter roars.

And then Kiera moves away from me.

"Adam, enough!" she shouts.

Adam is beside her in an instant, and Drake looks between her and him with narrowed eyes. "You know this *mutant*?"

"His name is Adam," Kiera's voice has taken on a cold tone, "and if you can't speak to him like a person, you won't speak to me either."

Drake looks surprised, but I'm not. Kiera was like this as a girl too. A child with a strong moral compass, with a sure sense of right and wrong. And she didn't back down from anyone, not even a dragon shifter.

I rise from my knees, back in my human form.

Kiera's gaze snaps back to me. "What are you doing here?"

I lift my hands in a motion of surrender. "I'm here to help."

"I don't think I can handle any more of your *help*."

Despite everything I've been through in my life, her words make me flinch. She was right. From the moment I came back into her life, I'd ruined it. "Once you're safe, I'm gone. I promise."

"Safe? With the 'king'?" she asks, her voice filled with sarcasm.

"You might not believe this, but I'm trying to keep you safe *from* him."

"I thought it was your plan to give me to him?"

I run the backs of my fingers along my beard, trying, unsuccessfully, to calm myself. To find the right words. "I understand if you don't trust me, but that's because you don't understand."

Her stunning blue eyes hold mine. "I understand that you disappeared from my life and then reappeared long enough to turn it upside down."

"Kiera—"

"Where did you go?"

I don't want to tell her.

"Did they not have phones?" Her words are like a slap.

"Fuck." I pace away from her. "I can't do this."

"You can't have a conversation? How unexpected!"

I press my hands against the cold stone, fighting for control. In the many years since she'd seen me last, I thought everything inside of me capable of feeling anything was dead. I'd thought Maxen had killed this side of myself. But now, with Kiera, it was like that other side of me was coming back to life.

And coming back to life hurt. Too much. Especially knowing that soon she'd be gone and I'd just have to die all over again to survive.

"Emory says he's come to save you from Mario," Adam says, completely unhelpfully.

"He also told Mario and his men he'd help return me to Maxen." Every one of her words are thrown at me like barbs. "And he *happens* to be Maxen's brother."

"Step-brother," I whisper. *Like it matters.*

Then she's there beside me, slamming her hand into my shoulder.

I turn to face her. The anger in those familiar eyes of hers makes my heart ache. I've wanted to see Kiera again, every day of my life. But I didn't want her to see *me*. I didn't want her to see who I'd become.

"You are the brother to a monster. You're the servant of a cruel piece of garbage."

What can I say? "Yes, I am."

"And then you come here acting like I should trust you?"

"Kiera—"

I'm surprised when tears spring to her eyes. She hits my shoulder again, and I turn to fully face her, overwhelmed by the pain in her eyes.

"You were my best friend. And you just left!"

"I didn't want to!" I find myself saying.

"Oh, really?"

"Yes!" And now I'm shouting. "My life was perfect with you! And then my mom's boyfriend left her, and she didn't want to have some kid to take care of anymore. I didn't even know where we were going. I couldn't comprehend the horror of her leaving me in a strange house, with a strange man she said was my father. It was the first of the many worst moments of my life! But nothing, nothing compares to seeing you that day with the vampires! Nothing!"

A tear escapes and trails down her cheek. "I don't believe you."

I grab her by the shoulders and drag her against me. "Look at me."

When her gaze leaves my face, I snatch her chin and drag her back.

"Do I look like a man who's lying?"

Those eyes of hers weigh me, and I can't breathe. I can't speak. All I can do is look into her eyes and wait for her to hurt me again.

"Oh, Emory." When she gathers me into her arms, I

don't expect it. And I don't know what to do. My mind searches for the last time anyone hugged me. For the last time someone cared enough to try to comfort me.

But…I can't recall.

When she draws back from me, I see that more tears have fallen. "What are we going to do?"

I take a deep breath, pushing down the tightness in my chest. "You have to understand. The prophecy says that whoever you marry will be king. Being the real king is all Maxen has ever wanted." I take another deep breath to swallow down the image of Kiera anywhere near that monster. "You will be in danger forever. Wherever you go. You'll need to just keep running and never look back."

"Or we kill him."

I glance up to see the dragon shifter watching us, and there's a coldness to his expression that surprises me. Could he really see her as his mate? For some reason, I didn't believe it until now.

"He's too well-protected," I say. "He's surrounded himself with the most violent group of thugs you could imagine. I don't think the three of us could kill him."

"Four of us," the mutant says, softly.

Kiera draws back from me, and she moves to Adam, pulling him into her arms. When she draws back, she strokes his cheek. "Adam, I told you that you were special to me. But I can't draw you into this. Any life with me would just be running and hiding and—"

"There is no life without you," he says.

Pain dances on her face. "You barely know me."

"I know enough."

She looks at all of us. "None of you really know me."

"You're my mate," Drake says, as if he was mentioning the weather.

"You're my family," Adam adds, and I swear her heart breaks when she hears the words.

Then they look at me.

I don't have any sweet words for her. I don't have any claims that this is something more than the situation. I only have the truth.

"All of this is my fault. I couldn't live with myself if I abandoned you now. And I'm also the only one who knows my brother well enough to keep you safe from him."

She looks troubled. "So what's the plan?"

"We killed the berserkers who wanted to hurt you," Adam says.

"All of them?" I ask, surprised.

He nods, and I make a mental note to ask him how the hell he managed that.

"Then she's safe here…for a little while. Until he hires his next goons to go after her."

They all look at me, waiting for a plan.

"But it won't be long before someone else tries to hurt her," Drake says.

"Yes, but I'm not sure if she'll be safer in or out of the reform school."

And then we look at Kiera.

She releases a slow breath. "I say, for now, we stay here. We come up with a better plan. And when the right opportunity comes along, we break free." She looks at us. "If that's what you want."

Drake shrugs. "I was never graduating as a dragon shifter."

"Nor was I as a mutant," Adam says.

Then all eyes are on me. "I was going to stay here, out of my brother's grasp forever. But I was stupid to think I was safe here." My words come out surprisingly bitter. "So, I'll go wherever you go."

Kiera smiles. "Then we have a plan."

I don't tell her it's not a very good one. That no plan will likely save her from my brother, because something dawns on me. Something she isn't ready to hear.

There might be a way to ensure that she stays safe forever.

We just have to find a berserker lord to marry her.

It solves all our problems. I'll have to suggest it. But as she leads us to the water to clean up after our fight, I can't find the words. Because as much as I want to tell myself this is all about making us even, I can't imagine Kiera with another man.

Hell. She truly has made me human again.

Chapter Twenty-One

KIERA

Four days after I was placed in the detention cells, a golem came for my body. When he found me alone in the building, all the flesh eaters dead, my men hidden until they could spring free behind me, he grunted and led me right back out. People gaped at me as I walked back to the House of Berserkers.

Everyone, it seemed, had thought I'd die with the flesh eaters.

I wished I could admit to them that I wasn't the badass they thought I was. That a giant dragon had torn the flesh eaters to shreds without me having to lift a finger. But then, the participation in my punishment by Adam, Emory, and Drake was a secret.

So, I returned to my room, bathed, and headed to the dining hall for lunch.

Inside, I spotted Emory and Drake at a table. They paused in their conversation as I approached, and both men tracked my movements as I went through the serving line.

When I reached the end, I heard murmuring rise up

from near the start of the line. My gaze snapped in the direction. Adam stood in the line, looking confused, wearing torn shorts and a worn white shirt. His feet were bare. His gaze uneasy.

But my heart sang.

Hurrying to the table with Drake and Emory, I set my tray down and rushed to where Adam stood in line. The angry mumbles about the "mutant" seemed to rise up from all directions. When he picked up a tray, a vampire in front of him smacked it out of his hand, and the plastic tray hit the floor with a sound that silenced the room.

To my surprise, Adam simply reaches for the next tray. But the second he picks it up, the vampire smacks it out of his hands again.

Cold fury unravels inside of me.

A big shifter bumps Adam from behind, and the vampire looms over him. I can feel the bloodlust in the air as the students watch, waiting for Adam to be hurt. Unfortunately for them, my own bloodlust was rising, my vision going red. I have to take several breaths before I can calm myself enough not to attack.

But then I'm there. "What's your problem?"

The vampire glances at me, and his gaze slides down my body. "How about I beat the shit out of this mutant and then we go have a roll?"

"Have a roll?" Adam frowns in confusion.

"You're going to leave him alone," I say, a warning in my voice, as I continue to think of puppies, rainbows, and all the shit my mom had always told my brothers to think about when they were losing control.

The vampire's eyes widen in surprise. "You're trying to protect...*it*? The fucking mutant?"

"His name is Adam." I feel myself swelling, and realize the puppies and rainbows aren't cutting it. So, I try to find my goddamn happy place. But the image of my candlelit room and my lucky vibrator feels far away.

If I ever talk to my brothers again, I'm going to have to apologize. This calming shit is harder than I thought.

"Why does he want a roll with you?" Adam asks again, looking from me to the man.

I move closer, squaring off with the vampire. "Go get your food and let him get his food, and no one needs to get hurt."

The shifter grins. "Sweetheart, you're pretty, but dumb. Mutants aren't people. They don't have names. They don't know how to eat in a cafeteria. They're like animals." I open my mouth to speak, but he keeps going. "But you don't need to be smart for me to fuck you."

Adam tilts his head and his eyes narrow. "What did you just say to her?"

I grab the vampire by the shirt and slam him back against the cafeteria line. "I'm going to smack the ignorance right out of you."

The shifter behind Adam suddenly grabs him by the shirt. "This isn't your fight, female. Now, mutant, how about I show you the door?"

"There a problem?" comes from behind me, the deep, threatening voice rolling down my spine and settling between my thighs.

The shifter springs back from Adam. "No, sir. No problem."

Drake moves closer to the shifter, and the man lowers his head in a show of submission, even though at full height Drake completely dwarfs him. "Anyone bothers the woman or the mutant, then they have a problem with me."

The room goes completely silent.

"Understand?" he barks, and I swear the other shifters jerk.

The vampire dares to smirk. "I'm just going to find a moment when your big, bad bodyguard isn't with you to teach you a lesson."

I didn't know Emory was there until he grabs the vampire by the back of the hair. He slams his face into the metal bars of the cafeteria furniture four times in rapid succession, and then releases the vampire as he slides to the ground. All along, he manages to keep from going berserk, but I can see the fury in his eyes.

"I wanted to do that," I growl at both the big men, my own anger still rolling beneath my flesh.

Adam cocks his head, a question in his eyes.

"Yes?" Drake asks, lifting a brow.

"You two protected me."

Drake shrugs, rolling those massive shoulders of his. "If Kiera wants you safe, you stay safe."

Adam smiles. "We're friends."

"I didn't say--"

"Friends," he repeats, then steps over the vampire and takes his tray. Everyone in line clears out of his way, and he looks pleased as he goes through the line, selecting different things. The cafeteria ladies scoop food onto his plate without hesitation, and then he heads for the table.

We follow him, Emory and Drake at my sides. "Thanks," I say, unable to look away from the happiness in Adam's face.

"We'll always keep you safe," Emory tells me softly.

"Oh, I didn't need help, but I like Adam knowing you have his back."

I feel the two men exchange a look over my head, but I don't even care.

"We just want to keep you happy," Drake says, but there's a note to his voice I haven't heard before.

I try to hide my smile. "Well, there's nothing that turns

me on more than seeing two sexy men beating the hell out of bullies."

Their surprise is almost palpable.

"Well then, I'll strive to beat up more men for you."

When we reach our table, I turn to face Drake, grinning. I know he doesn't suspect it before I land a hard kiss to those perfect lips of his. But just as the flame of desire leaps into his eyes and his hands reach for me, I leap back and take my seat next to Adam.

Drake makes a sound of frustration as he sits down across from me.

Adam smiles at all of us. "That was kind of fun."

Emory makes a grumpy noise, but I know there's a smile behind his frown.

Then Adam sighs. "I haven't had warm food in so long. Everything looks so good."

My heart aches a little at his words. "Well, eat as much as you want, and we can go back for seconds."

Adam digs into the food and speaks around a chunk of meat. "This is the best day of my life." I open my mouth to respond to him, but he adds, "Except the day we had sex."

I feel my cheeks burning and take a big bite of my food.

Drake makes a low sound that sounds like a threat. "About that…is the mutant the only one getting to see you naked?"

I swallow my food and drink some of my soda before answering. I plan to say something clever and flirtatious, but when our eyes meet, the words die on my lips. "You keep not being a jerk and see where it gets you."

He flashes me a wicked smile. "Challenge accepted."

I'm about to tell him that it wasn't a challenge when I see Emory staring at me. The longing in his eyes takes my breath away. But when he sees me looking at him, he draws his gaze away and focuses on his food.

I eat the rest of my meal in silence, feeling troubled. Drake and Adam had made their motivations clear. But Emory seems to think he has to protect me because of some strange pride, or like he has a debt to me. But was it something more?

Somehow I'd imagined…I'd thought that there was more to the mysterious man who saved me that day. Or maybe I just wanted there to be. And now that I knew that he and Emory were the same, it had changed something inside of me. Every time I thought of him, my emotions felt super charged. Complicated.

And I didn't like complicated.

Chapter Twenty-Two

DRAKE

For three days, life was calm…or as calm as it could be at the Wicked Reform School. We took our classes. A wolf shifter librarian took over for our Fighting teacher, and I was proud to show Kiera some new moves without the threat of some asshole teacher putting her in a dangerous position.

As a wrestling partner, she was…surprisingly capable. I mean, it didn't hurt that every time she touched me all my blood went straight to my cock. But even so, she impressed me.

And then there was the day she fought a shifter, him with a sword and her with those fucking axes of hers. To say it was amazing was an understatement. She used the deadly blades like they were an extension of herself. The shifter had been on his back, the blades to his throat, before he'd known what hit him.

Now she wore the things on her back at all times. And as much as I hated to admit it, the sight of them got me hard.

Which was just…fucked up.

I shiver, trying to push the thought of just how good Kiera was with her hands out of my mind.

The mutant had chosen to shadow Emory in all his classes, for some reason, but had managed not to have to fight in class so far, so I still had no idea what he was capable of. Most of the time, he seemed more fascinated by the interactions of everyone in the class than the lesson that was taught.

Not that I blamed him, he seemed to know nothing about other people.

And then there was Emory. I couldn't quite resist measuring the two men as my competition. While Kiera seemed to dote on Adam, and he received more attention than both of us combined, it was how little Emory and Kiera talked that bothered me. It was the way he looked at her when he thought no one was watching.

Never before had I imagined I'd share my mate. But if I had to, I would be certain of my place among her men. I refused to be the lowest male in her regard.

And yet, I still hadn't found a way to win her affection.

As I lazily wandered the forest near the cliffs, a sound made me freeze. There were people just up ahead. Angry people.

For a second, I intended to simply walk away. Not every fight was *my* fight, but then I heard the unmistakable sound of Adam's voice and cursed. The man seemed to find trouble everywhere he went.

Moving more quietly, I slide through the trees and spot four warlocks surrounding Adam. In his hands, he holds wildflowers, no doubt gathered for Kiera. And his face is troubled.

"I didn't know these were your woods," he says.

One of the warlocks, a man with long red hair, grins, then murmurs beneath his breath. A second later, flames leap from his fingertips, burning the flowers in Adam's hand.

The mutant gasps and drops the bunch onto the ground. "Why did you do that?"

"Because," the warlock advances on the mutant, even though Adam is easily double his size, "we don't want you here."

Adam frowns, but his words came out soft, "Then I'll leave the woods."

He starts to walk away, but another warlock blocks his path.

Adam looks startled.

The red-head grins. "I don't think you understand. We don't want you at our reform school."

The mutant draws himself up taller. "Kiera wants me here, so I'm staying here."

All the assholes start to laugh, but it's the red-head who responds. "Mutants are basically just test animals, right? How about we do some tests of our own? How about we try out some spells on you?"

Adam goes white. I might be a cold-hearted bastard, but the terror on his face tears at my own heart strings. "I don't like tests."

"And you won't like ours either," the warlock says, a savage promise in his words.

I emerge from the trees. "Warlocks in the woods. Strange. I'd have thought there was a dark hole you should be casting spells in."

All of them whirl around, and I finally recognize the red-head as Harold, a douchebag who was apparently an expert caster. "This isn't your fight, lizard."

"That's king of the shifters to you, asshole," I snarl.

Something dangerous swims in his dark eyes. "I noticed

that you chose to live with the shifters, while the House of Dragons stands empty. Why is that?"

A growl slips from my lips, and I try to push back the memories of my first day on campus. Of coming to that quiet building. The walls lined with photos of powerful, dead dragons. The last of the photos was an image of my own parents.

"Afraid of the ghosts?"

My hands curl into fists.

"Careful," he threatens, "even dragons aren't immune to my powers."

"Even warlocks can burn," I threaten back.

His gaze grows calculating. "I heard they destroyed your wings and cut off your cock. I heard they left you half a dragon."

My entire chest aches as the memories of that day rise within me. And I know I take too long to respond.

"Don't hurt my friend's feelings," Adam says, his words quiet but angry.

The warlocks glance from me to him, and then they start laughing. "A mutant and a dickless, wingless dragon! How perfect!"

I planned to destroy them, but Adam was faster. Claws emerge from his hands, and he slashes Harold's face. The warlock screams and my jaw drops as Adam picks him up, lifting him over his head. He races through the trees and I see him toss the asshole off the cliff, into the ocean far below. When he turns to face us, his eyes glow golden.

One warlock starts to murmur a spell. I punch him in the face, watching the bastard crumble into an unconscious heap. When I look up, Adam is dragging the last two warlocks to the cliff. As they scream the words to spells I don't understand, I feel magic brewing around them, but

Adam simply tosses them over the edge, completely unaffected by their dark powers.

I'm grinning when I go to stand next to him. We watch until we see three shapes emerge from the water down far below. I don't tell Adam he just made himself some powerful enemies, because I wouldn't say a thing to ruin this moment. The quiet mutant had actually grown a backbone and fought back!

"That was…good, mutant."

The glow in Adam's eyes fades. "They hurt your feelings."

Is that why he fought? The thought bothers me for reasons I don't understand.

I rub my back, then stop myself when I realize what I'm doing. "I'm fine. Don't worry."

His gaze meets mine. "Did they really cut off your dick and your wings?"

I sigh. "Half of that is true."

He looks at my groin.

"My wings!"

His gaze jerks up. "I'm sorry. Did it hurt?"

I swear I haven't ever admitted something hurt before. "Yes. More than anything in my life."

Adam tries to take my hand.

I spring back. "What are you doing?"

He looks confused. "Kiera holds my hand when I'm sad."

"Dudes don't do that…"

"So what do they do?"

"I don't know." I run my hands through my hair in frustration, then curse myself when I realize I've messed up my hair. "I don't usually see a purpose in having men as friends. Hell, usually I don't see a use for women other than…well, so, I think dudes just pat each other on the back."

Adam's expression grows serious. He walks up to me very slowly, then pats me lightly on the back.

I can't help but laugh. "Come on, let's get you back before Kiera worries."

We leave the woods and run into Kiera and Emory just outside of the berserker house. Neither of them are talking. They just sit next to each other on the steps, looking opposite directions. He with a sword on his back, her with her axes. It's a strange sight. Like they're the same but different all at once.

When they spot us, Kiera springs to her feet. "Where have you been?"

Adam's expression falls. "I was gathering you flowers, but the warlocks burned them."

Her hand goes to the hilt of one of the axes of her back. "What warlocks? What happened?"

Adam smiles. "Drake, my friend, beat them up for me. Then I patted his back when they hurt his feelings. They said he didn't have a dick or wings, but only half of that was true."

Kiera and Emory look at my crotch.

"My cock is just fine!" I growl.

And then Kiera laughs, dropping her hand from her weapon. *Was she just screwing with my head?*

I feel some of my tension ease away.

"Don't we have history class now?" Adam asks Emory.

The berserker looks resigned as he says, "Yes, I guess *we* do."

They take off, both casting Kiera glances as they do so. My gaze moves back to Kiera, and I find her watching me, those blue eyes of hers evaluating me. I stand absolutely still and let her look, wondering what she's thinking. And having absolutely no clue.

"I have a break between classes," she says.

I lift a brow. I already knew that. "We both do."

"I was thinking of doing some laps in the lake by the mermaid house. It's usually quiet this time of day. Want to come with me?"

I nod.

But instead of going to get a bathing suit, she starts heading in the direction of the lake. I forget to move until she looks back at me and grins, and then I'm hurrying after her, falling in line beside her.

"So, you protected Adam?"

I shrug. "Not that he needed it. The mutant can handle himself better than I suspected."

"I heard rumors they found the bodies of some berserkers in the detention house. They said the men must have broken into it and been attacked by flesh eaters."

"Adam and Emory are more useful than I initially thought."

She studies me from beneath her lashes. "So, you like them?"

"Like isn't exactly the word I'd use. I…tolerate them for you."

She looks disappointed.

I instantly regret my words. "I don't like when people are unkind to Adam. I've never understood people who are cruel just to be cruel. And Emory, he's hard to read."

"He's different from when we were kids."

"I don't know what he was like then, but it sounds like he endured some pretty bad things. If half the stories about his brother are true, it's probably even worse than he said. I wouldn't be surprised if he changed. Bad things have a way of turning us into people we never imagined."

Kiera surprises me by slipping her hand in mine. "I wonder what it means that I've had a good life."

I'm careful not to do anything that makes her draw her hand back. "You don't have to be as fucked up as the three of us to be a good person. And actually, maybe that's why we seem drawn to you; you *aren't* jaded. You're…different."

"I don't think Emory is drawn to me," she says, frowning.

Does she really not see it? "Trust me, he is."

She studies me. "What makes you say that?"

I debate not telling her, but then sigh and decide the hell with it. "He looks at you the same way I look at you."

"And how do you look at me?"

We stop at the edge of the lake. Turning, I catch her gaze. Looking at our hands, still entwined, I stroke the top of her hand and try to think of my response.

"This whole mate thing…you don't really know me. How do you know that there's really something between us?"

It's hard to breathe as I choose my words carefully. "It's like…knowing that the sun will rise in the morning. Never before has a shifter chosen a mate who was wrong for them. The fact that my dragon chose you means that you're the female for me. There is no other."

"I thought you were only pretty sure I was your mate."

I draw closer. "I lied."

And then I lean down, and she surprises me by kissing me. At first, our kiss is soft, and then it grows harder and more desperate. My hands run down her shoulders and arms, then grab her hips and pull her closer. Her hands dig into my hair, pulling me down to her, and she takes control of our kiss.

I never let women take control of me, but I let Kiera. It's fascinating to feel how she angles me. To see how her tongue guides mine. And yet, the desire inside of me grows hotter until it threatens to unleash.

With other women, I wouldn't have held back. With her, I do.

I *will not* screw this up.

When she breaks our kiss, she's breathing hard. "That was…"

She doesn't need to say more. That kiss was better than good. It was everything.

"Come on," she whispers.

We walk the outside of the lake until it curves into the woods. She takes us through some trees to a quieter part of the lake, then turns back to me. "Ready to swim?"

My mouth goes dry, but I nod.

She takes off the sheath with her weapons and then her black tank top, dropping both onto a rock. The black bra she wears underneath is sexy as hell, thin, and made of silk. My fingers itch to take it off, but then she draws off her boots and pants, and stands before me in just her bra and underwear.

"Your turn."

I don't hesitate. I reach for the hem of my shirt and strip the material off slowly, giving her a full view of my six pack, and my arms…the ones women are always complimenting. And by the way her gaze glides over me, Kiera likes what she sees too.

When I take off everything except my boxers, I stand before her, feeling proud. This woman is beautiful, more beautiful than any woman I've ever seen, but I'm a man who can stand at her side. If she'll let me.

"Come on," she says, and then she turns, darting into the water.

I follow after her, more slowly, watching the way her

underwear hugs the glorious curves of her ass. "That's spectacular."

She looks back at me as she sinks into the water. "What?"

"Your ass."

She grins. "Thanks."

"Ever had a cock in it?"

I expect her to blush. I expect her to ignore me. But instead, she lifts a brow. "Enough times to know I like it, when the man knows what he's doing."

Catching her around the waist in the water, I draw her closer. "Well, I know what I'm doing."

"You sure?"

"How about I show you?"

Her expression grows uncertain.

"Or are you all talk?"

"I'm not all talk, but I'm guessing you are."

I chuckle, and my laugh comes out low and aroused. Turning her around, I push her forward into the water, not caring that the water still has a lingering chill beneath the shadows of the forest.

When the water covers her chest, and she shivers in front of me, I stop. One of my hands stays on her hips, and my other hand slides down her belly. I feel her stomach muscles clench, and then I keep going down. Slipping my hand beneath the silky material of her underwear, I let my fingers run over her smooth mound, and love the way she shivers.

I watch her breathing grow more rapid, and her head falls back against me in a way that has my blood boiling.

Parting her folds, I use one finger to work the softness of her body, learning what she likes, and what she likes more. This woman might think I'm arrogant, but I'm not.

I'm confident, because if there's one thing I know how to do, it's please a woman.

I use all my fingers to stroke her, to touch her, lightly, and I know by the way she jerks that her body wants more. That she wants me to move faster. But if there's one thing a woman needs, it's her desire built up. She needs to be wound up so tightly that when she finally comes, it's like an earthquake.

And so, I touch her, my own cock hard as I picture replacing my fingers with my cock. As it bounces against her ass, longing for more.

At last, I push one of my fingers into her channel, and she gasps. I ease it into her slick body until I'm deep, then slowly draw back out. Over and over again until her entire body is shaking.

She doesn't need to tell me to add another finger. I do. And I slide my hand from her hips to her breasts. Drawing the material off, I pull her breasts free and glory in the sight of them just below the water. I was right. She's perfect. Her breasts are fucking full.

When I pinch one of her nipples, her knees almost buckle. I tug her ass back against my hard cock, then return to her breasts. I fondle them as my fingers continue to ease in and out of her, claiming the woman as my own. I long to flip her around and taste her breasts, but I tell myself that all good things come to those who wait.

Taking my hand from her breasts, I slide my fingers into the back of her underwear and continue to watch her breasts bounce as I add another finger into that tight pussy of hers. I feel her tense as I tease her from behind, then gently push one finger into her ass.

She's breathing hard. Those gorgeous breasts of hers seem to swell with each breath.

Kissing my way down her throat, I suck on the junction

between her throat and shoulders and love the way she shudders. Four fingers move in and out of her pussy with slow, deliberate movements, and I manage to slide one finger all the way into her ass. A moan slips past her lips, and I smile against her throat.

Drawing my finger out, I add another one and work her ass, preparing it for my cock. Listening to the signs her body gives, pushing harder when she needs it, going softer when she needs it. By the time I have four fingers in her ass and four in her pussy, she's wrapped her arm around one of mine, keeping herself from falling.

Finally, she groans, "Drake, please."

I bite her throat lightly. "Please what?"

"Come on." She wiggles against me, shuddering.

"What?"

"Fuck my ass," she begs, her request a rush of breath.

My control nearly snaps, and it's my turn to shudder. I pull my fingers out of her ass, tug her underwear and my boxers down. Keeping one hand buried in her pussy, I use the other one to part her from behind and slowly ease inside of her.

I'm big, and she's fucking tight, but I've prepared her sweet ass perfectly. Going slowly, I keep going until I reach my hilt, and then we're both breathing hard together.

Grasping her hip with one hand, and keeping my other hand in her pussy, I slowly begin to fuck her from behind. Usually this is the time when I listen to a woman's pleasure, and wait for my own, like waiting for a steak to cook. But this fucking with Kiera is nothing like that. It's my own body that screams for release. It's every nerve in my cock that feels every inch of her body.

My vision wavers, and I start to fuck her harder. She wraps her hands around my wrist and rubs against my hand as I take her, lost to my desire. Lost to the pleasure of this moment between my mate and I.

When she starts to chant my name, I almost come undone. But I manage to keep control long enough to work us both into a frenzy, and then she crashes over the edge, her scream tearing into the silence of the lake. Seconds later, I come too, filling her sweet ass with my hot cum.

I don't stop until we've both finished riding the waves of our pleasure, and then I finally calm. My heart is racing. Normally, this is when I'd pull away from a woman, find my clothes, and be gone. But I don't do that now. I keep my cock deep inside her, and my fingers buried in her, and I love the way our hearts seem to beat as one.

This woman…she's mine, whether she's accepted it or not.

She tugs my hand out of her, and then slides forward until my cock comes out. When she turns around, I'm spellbound by her.

I cross the space between us and kiss her harder. I kiss her until I have to stop to draw in a breath.

She sags against me, gasping for breath. "That was…"

"Good?"

She laughs, her laugh husky. "Better than good. Much better."

I stroke her hair and kiss her head. "I'm glad."

I didn't care that students could've been walking through the woods, or that the lake wasn't entirely secluded. I wanted to hold her forever. I wanted this moment to last forever.

But she eventually pulls back. "We have class soon."

"I don't give a fuck."

She laughs. "I know, but we can't just stay here."

"Can't we?" And I hate that I desperately want her to say yes.

She wraps me in her arms and kisses my chin. "If it helps, you lived up to all my expectations and more."

My chest seems to swell. "Did I?"

She kisses my lips lightly. "All of them."

When she fixes her bra and heads back for shore, I watch her with longing. There was a time when Kiera would be like a dragon queen. She would rule over my family's lands, with me at her side. She would have anything and everything she ever wanted.

It killed me that she was little more than a prisoner. That we both were. And that our only hope of getting free was to depend on a berserker I wasn't even sure I trusted.

That's the moment it hits me. Staring at her as she leaves me. I need…I need to try to fly again. I didn't want to test my wings. I didn't want to know if they could never work again. I didn't want any of the students here to see me fail.

But for Kiera…for Kiera I'll swallow my pride and my fear.

For Kiera, I would give anything. Even this.

Chapter Twenty-Three

KIERA

Cora, the school psychiatrist, sits across from me, reading a file in her lap. I know it has to be the notes from our last three sessions, and I know that soon her careful questions will begin again. The woman with the strawberry blonde hair wears an expensive red suit that's oddly elegant, and stunning red high-heels. If I didn't dislike her so much, I might envy her sense of fashion.

But the truth was that I didn't just not like her, I also didn't *trust* her, which was sort of a requirement of a good psychiatrist. Something about her made me feel uneasy. Maybe it was because, after surviving the flesh eaters a couple weeks ago, I'd been required to come here. Or maybe it was just because I'm sensing more and more other students at the school watching me too closely, and it's kind of fried my nerves.

At last, that too-sweet smile of hers appears, and she sets the file down in her lap, those big hazel eyes of hers drinking me in. "Well, Kiera, it seems since the episode with your teacher, things have gone fairly well for you at the school."

"Yeah, I guess."

"Fighting, gardening, history, math, English, and your special subjects...none of your teachers have had a single complaint about you. Which, you have to imagine, is unusual for a berserker."

I'm surprised. "It is?"

She nods. "Most of you...go berserk eventually. You see, what happened with your Fighting teacher, that's a bit of a grey zone. He forced you to lose control, he was hurt as a result, and you survived your punishment. In the eyes of the dean and the staff, your slate is...washed clean. But most berserkers lose control at inopportune moments. People get hurt, and they prove exactly why they were sent here."

My heart beats far too quickly. I'd heard stories about other berserkers losing it. Apparently, the detention centers had different kinds of punishments in them, depending on the crime. And witches used their powers to switch the types of punishment. So one day building number one had flesh eaters and a deep staircase, and the next a room full of water with sheer sides. Students spent days trying to keep their heads above water. Sometimes they lived. Sometimes they died. And then the next week? A new punishment might take place in the same building.

Some of the berserkers disappeared for a few days and reappeared looking exhausted. Some looked terrified. Others acted as if they might only be holding onto their sanity by a thread.

And then there were the berserkers that never came back.

"I want to graduate," I say.

Her lips curl into a smile I don't like for a second before it fades. "Well, there's a first time for everything."

"Berserkers never graduate?" *Were they right? Do I not even have a chance?*

"I usually don't say never…but no, I don't believe any have. If we catch them losing control, even if they do well the rest of their time here, they're usually executed at graduation."

"That doesn't seem fair."

"Fair?" She lifts a brow. "What's not fair is that most of you had to do some pretty horrible shit to end up here, Kiera, and for some reason society deems it necessary to give most of the youth another chance. Even though, let's be frank, most of you don't deserve it."

"That's a great attitude for a *counselor* here."

She leans back in her chair, her red suit no longer as elegant as I first thought when I entered the room. Instead, it reminds me of the kind of outfit a devil-woman might wear. "I got an interesting call the other day. From a Lord Maxen. Any idea what he wanted?"

Shit. That takes me by surprise, but I try to recover quickly. "Me as his bride."

She smiles. "You surprise me, Kiera. You're smart for a berserker. Yes, he wanted to enlist my help to break you free."

I let the not-so-subtle insult about my people's intelligence go. "Why are you telling me this?"

"Because I didn't take his deal. I'm a bit above his pay grade, but I bet there are others here on his payroll."

I think of the dead berserkers and clench my teeth together. The school blamed the flesh eaters for their deaths; the last thing I wanted was to put any suspicion on me and the guys. So, I say nothing.

She lifts a brow. "Nothing to say? Okay then, how about we talk about Emory?"

Again, I'm surprised. *How does she know about Emory and*

I? Yeah, we've continued to eat together with Adam and Drake. And yes, he tended to stand near me in the classes we had together, but no, I wouldn't think the counselor would know anything about him and I.

"He's Lord Maxen's brother, right? The bastard?"

I draw myself up taller, and glance at the little waterfall on the table next to her. I'm disliking this room and this woman more with each second that passes. "I don't really have anything to say about him."

"No? Well, it just seems strange to me that you had a get out of jail free card from Lord Maxen, that you refused, and yet you've allowed his little minion to get so close to you."

"You don't understand," I say, glaring at that damned fountain.

"Oh? Did the big, sexy berserker give you some sob story? Emory isn't the first of Lord Maxen's men to arrive here. Far more berserkers come from his house than all the houses combined. But do you know what I've learned about them after all this time?"

I hate that I want to know. "What?"

"He has those bastards so fucking brainwashed that they'll lay out their neck on the chopping block for him. I don't know how the hell anyone can create that type of loyalty. I've done some…experiments myself, and it seems it takes years."

"Why are you telling me this?"

There's a smile in her eyes. "Because, Kiera, I like you. And I don't like many students. Berserkers especially. But I've read your story…about the vampires and your best friend. I actually think you could return to the real world and maybe not be a stain on society. The only thing that makes me doubt you is how stupid you are to trust one of Maxen's men."

"He's not like them."

She lifts a brow.

I clench my hands together, and I hate that I feel a ripple under my skin. Taking deep breaths, I will that side of me to calm. I will the beast within to remember that we can't just lose our shit every time something upsets us.

When I can breathe easily again, I try to explain, without saying too much. "I trust him. We…have a history together."

"And you believe this history is enough to undo the years spent breaking him down and building him into the perfect soldier by a twisted leader?" She laughs. "You're either stupid, Kiera, or too cocky for your own good."

"I trust him," I say again, but we can both hear the doubt in my voice.

She opens her mouth to say more, but the phone by her damned water fountain rings. Frowning, she picks it up, "I'm in session you mindless, clay piece of…what? Alright then."

Her gaze is filled with hatred as she sets down her phone. "Well, it seems our session will have to end early today. You're wanted in the library."

"Wanted? By who?"

Her teeth clench together for a second. "I believe that whore librarian, Ms. Farah herself."

I stand in one smooth motion. I've never been in the library, nor have I met the librarian. But I'm pretty sure I'd rather be anywhere than here, having this woman shine a light on the dark fears in my heart.

"Thank you," I say.

She smiles, opens her file, and begins to write.

I head for the door, but her voice stops me. "See, most berserkers are beasts without manners. You, Kiera, are something else altogether. And I intend to figure you out before graduation."

I shiver. For some reason, her words sound like a threat.

Leaving her office, I headout of the building and step into the main courtyard of the reform school. For some reason, my legs are shaking. I take a second to sit down on the edge of the fountain, taking deep breaths. The counselor was a colossal bitch, but could she be right about Emory? Or was Drake right when he said there was something more between Emory and I?

Emory seemed to care for me, but he was so damned hard to read. Maybe he was just sticking around out of guilt. He *was* the one that brought those vampire beasts to our area. But at the same time, didn't it make more sense that his brother had asked him to stay close to me?

I sigh. *But then, he killed the other berserkers. Why would he do that if he was working for Maxen?*

Frustrated, I ran my hands lazily through the fountain, my thoughts drifting. My gaze moves over the few students that walk through the courtyard. A couple shifters, females, that seem like they might be bird shifters, laugh together. A vampire holds his head high, even though he wears a dark robe that protects his delicate skin from the sun, until he walks out of view. I stiffen when a nephilim steps out of a building. I can always pick out the angels. They're beautiful, but not the normal kind of beautiful. They seem to glow. And something about them makes me feel like my eyes are tricking me into thinking they're more beautiful than they actually are.

"Ouch!"

Yanking my hand out of the water, I turn and spot a small hippocampus in the water. The horse's pale white body glimmers with blue and purple, and its horse-like head dips through the water like it's racing. And yet, it seems to be lingering around where I sit.

"What'd I ever do to you?" I ask it, frowning.

They're just jerks.

I jump a little as the voice enters my mind. Heart racing, I glance around the courtyard. A phoenix male gives me a cocky wink just before entering a building, but there's no one around that I can imagine capable of putting words into my mind.

Up here.

"Up where?"

The tree by the psychologist's window.

My gaze slides to the tree not twenty feet from me. For a minute I don't see anything, and then I spot the mangy cat. Truly, I don't think I've ever seen a cat look as wild as this one. His fur was every shade all at once, brown, orange, white, and grey, the colors merging together in the strangest way. And yet, I had to admit, I had a soft spot for cats. Even the one currently studying me, his tail twitching behind him.

"You must be the cat that Adam doesn't own."

His voice comes begrudgingly in my mind. *I am called Princess.*

"It's nice to meet you."

Be careful, berserker. You're being followed.

I stiffen and look around the courtyard again, but see no one.

"Who?"

You're being watched. Best to get going. Then the cat leaps gracefully down the branches and trots off.

I stand and try to look casual as I head for the library, but every nerve in my body is singing. Over the last couple of weeks, Adam and I have continued to get closer. He's spent most of his nights in my bed, except the nights Drake manages to claim it first. He didn't speak often of Princess, but when he did, I got the sense that he trusted the cat completely.

So I was going to go out on a limb and trust him too.

If he said someone was watching me, I had to assume someone was. Getting to the library, to a place with people, seemed like the smartest thing to do. Beside the fact that the librarian must be getting pissed about my little break before seeing her. So, I hightail it to the library, searching but seeing no one behind me.

I climb the stone steps of the big building and close the door quickly behind me. Instantly, I'm swallowed by silence. I pause in the doorway, looking at row after row of silent shelves, breathing in the musty scent of old books, and trying not to find the dim, flickering lights eerie. A part of me wants to turn around and go right outside. *Had I thought the library would seem safer?* Somehow, without the sounds of natural life outside, I felt even more uneasy.

Still, I walk slowly across the tiled floor, my boots sounding unnervingly loud in the silence. I come to a staircase. One way leads down. One way leads up. *Which way is the librarian?*

"Kiera?"

I spin around, instantly in a half-crouch, a hand on the hilt of one of my axes.

Behind me, a male nephilim stands. His golden hair has been cut short. His skin is a shocking milk-white, and his eyes are a deep brown. "Kiera, I've been waiting for you."

It's strange how fast I feel my body relax. I'd heard tales of how they could convince people to do what they wanted, how people felt compelled to obey them, but I'd never actually experienced it myself. Thoughts of the librarian and the cat's warning fade away, and there's only him and I.

"It's okay," he says, "you're safe with me. I'm the librarian's assistant. She sent me to find you."

My hand drops to my side and I rise. I try to speak, but I can't seem to think of anything to say.

"This way," he tells me, flashing his dimples.

I follow the glowing being down one set of stairs and then another. Somewhere in the back of my mind I'm aware that the temperature drops around me. A part of me knows that the lighting seems to grow even darker, and that that deep sense of silence seems to only grow deeper.

But I don't care. I follow him. This angel. Because I would follow him anywhere.

"This way," he calls behind him, but his long legs leave me behind.

I sprint to keep up, but he disappears from view behind a row of shelves.

Rushing to the row, I turn and stop short. Four male angels stand at the back of the dead end, the man who led me here among them. There's a sense of alarm ringing somewhere in my mind, but I remain where I am, staring at their brilliance.

"Kiera, King Maxen has grown impatient with you."

I stare, still somehow unable to speak.

"He asked us to bring you to him. To lead his wife to freedom. His men wait for you just beyond the gates. When they see us, they'll attack the guards, and you'll be free."

I try to push past the cloud that seems to hang over my mind. "I don't…I don't want…"

"You want freedom, right?" the blond asks me, drawing closer.

For the first time, I see the hilt of the sword at his back, and then I see the others. It means something to me, but I'm not sure what.

I stare at the angels. *Had they asked me a question?*

One of the angels lifts a grate in the floor, then they all look at me. The blond smiles again. "Come on, Kiera, we'll bring you to freedom."

I move forward.

Someone leaps out in front of me.

It takes too long for me to realize it's Emory. Breathing hard. His sword held out before him.

"Get out of here, Kiera," he orders.

The anger is his voice bothers me, although I can't quite be sure why.

I hear the blond angel laugh. "Berserker, this is a fool's errand. There are four of us and only one of you. This fight will be over before it starts."

"Kiera, run!"

I don't move. Instead, I shake my head. I close my eyes. In my thoughts, a calming melody seems to play, but Emory is disturbing the melody. Emory is making the world's colors brighter.

"Come on," the nephilim says, and now there's a purr in his words. "Put down your sword."

"Fuck off!" Emory shouts.

Another angel whispers, "Why isn't it working on him?"

"You aren't the first winged assholes I've fought," Emory hisses.

Fought? He's fighting them? Why?

"Come on, Kiera. Shake it off! It's just the damn angel spell!"

I swear I come crashing out of their spell, gasping for breath and shaking. They bespelled me? They were going to take me to Maxen? *Oh, fuck no...*

Reaching for the axes at my back, I slowly draw them from their sheaths. Moving closer, I come to stand at Emory's side.

"That was a mistake, flying rats," I growl.

The blond lifts an arrogant brow, and then they draw their swords from their sheaths.

We leap into battle like we've fought together a thousand times. Swords connect with my axes. Swords meet Emory's. But the primpy angels don't have a clue how to fight with our kind. They don't expect it when I kick one of them in the junk and knock his sword out of his hand. They don't expect it when I catch one sword with my axe and use the other one to lightly cut the back of a knee.

They might say our kind doesn't fight with honor. I say, we fight to win.

Within minutes, the angels are on their knees.

I hold an axe beneath the throat of two angels. Emory has his hovering in front of the blond, while the fourth lies out cold on the ground.

"Mercy," the blond begs.

I see fire in Emory's eyes as he draws his blade back to strike.

"Stop," I say.

Emory hesitates.

"They asked for mercy," I tell him, frowning.

We might fight to win, but we weren't the brutes that the other races thought. Honor was built into us from a young age. And I couldn't see anything honorable about killing people who have already surrendered.

He doesn't look at me as he answers. "They can't have mercy, Kiera. If they're working with my brother, this doesn't end until they're dead."

"No," the blond begs, no longer bothering with his lulling voice. "You let us walk away, and you have our word that we won't attack again. Please, there…there are so few of our kind."

"As there should be," Emory growls.

Part of me understands that what Emory says makes sense. Leaving potential enemies alive, especially ones as dangerous as the Nephilim, isn't logical. But I couldn't live with myself if I killed them in cold blood, and I needed to see exactly what Emory was capable of.

"I want your word," I snap.

"You have it," the angels all murmur at once.

I lower my axes.

"Kiera, no. You don't understand my brother! You don't understand the people who work for him!"

"It's over," I say, my gaze locking with his, daring him to defy me.

"No."

I sheath one of my axes and touch Emory's arm. "It's over."

For a minute, he seems to swell. And for the first time, I realize just how close he is to losing control. His muscles ripple beneath his skin.

Berserkers aren't exactly subtle when they're about to lose control during a fight. It surprises me that Emory can hide his bloodlust beneath an expressionless mask so easily. It's impressive… and worrisome.

Is he really just Maxen's brainwashed soldier? I couldn't believe that.

"Emory. For me…"

I'm surprised how quickly his blade moves from the angel's throat. "If I see any of you again, you're dead."

They scramble away, taking the unconscious body of the fourth angel with them, as if Emory might change his mind at any second and kill them right there. Which given the way he watches them, isn't out of the realm of possibilities.

I sheath my other axe and Emory slides his sword back onto his back. When he whirls toward me, complicated emotions flash across his face so fast that I can't follow them. "That was a mistake. They're not going to stop."

"I'm not killing men on their knees."

He swears and runs the back of his fingers along his beard, his jaw tense. "If you want to survive against Maxen, every fucking moral code, every fucking line you've learned not to cross, it all needs to be forgotten."

"Is that what you did?" I ask, half an accusation, half curious.

He lowers his gaze. "I did whatever I had to. And you need to learn to do the same, or you'll be his."

For some reason, anger rises inside of me. "You're not that guy, Emory!"

No, he wasn't. He wasn't some beaten-down man who served a master like a broken dog.

He draws back from me. "I am who I am."

I grab him by the shirt and drag him closer. His deep blue eyes meet mine, and there's surprise and longing in his gaze.

"You are Emory of the Winter Berserkers." He tries to draw back from me, shaking his head, but I yank him closer. "You're Emory of the Winter Berserkers. You're stronger than every man there. You're taller than any man there. But even as a boy, you liked the sunrise. You liked cold nights, and you thought bear tracks meant our ancestors were still watching over us."

His head falls. "Kiera. That side of myself…it's not there anymore. I'm not Emory, the boy you knew. I'm not Emory, a man who's grown into anyone of worth. I'm just…nothing anymore."

"Fuck that!"

I slam him back against the books, and he nearly loses his footing. "Kiera!"

And then I'm on him. I crush those soft lips of his under mine, and he returns my kiss with vigor. I press against him, and the second I do, I feel him harden.

He breaks our kiss, his gaze burning into mine. "We can't."

"Stop me," I say, then grab him by his hair, hard, and kiss him again.

His hands slide up and down the sides of my body, like he doesn't have a clue what to do, and I press my tongue into his mouth. His tongue tangles with my own, and something changes about our kiss.

I didn't know what I was doing. Punishing him for not being the man I thought he was? Proving that he wasn't the man he thought he was? Hell, maybe this had started out that way, but all of that had faded away. Now it was just Emory and I, wanting to ease the tension that's been building between us from the first moment we saw each other.

I know the moment he snaps. He shudders and turns us, pressing me against the bookshelf. My hand drops from his hair, and he continues to kiss me as if his life depends on it. One of his hands begins to work the button on my pants.

We're desperate as we tear off each other's pants, and my legs wrap around his back as he grabs my ass. Our kiss deepens. I rub against his length, begging him to plunge inside of me. But for a second he just kisses me, just presses against me, and my thoughts spin into nothingness. There's just a deep sense of pleasure, of getting what I need.

And then his hands tighten on my hips, and he adjusts me.

The head of his cock presses into my channel, and I gasp, my nails digging into his shoulders as he slides his massive length inside of me. For a minute, I can't seem to breathe. I almost tell him to stop. That he's too damned big for my body.

But then he reaches his hilt, and I break our kiss, holding myself still. And that tight feeling... it fades away until it feels so damn good. Not just having him inside of me. But knowing it's Emory inside of me.

He looks at me, and I catch his gaze. And for the first time, I realize just how messed up things were between us. Because even though he's looked at me a thousand times since he got here, I don't think he really *saw* me...or let me see him the way he does now.

He holds my gaze as he draws out of me and then plunges back in. We both cry out, and then he begins to fuck me. Slowly at first. Then faster and faster.

And all along, we look at each. Our eyes see into each other in a way that feels more intimate than fucking. It's a game of chicken. A game that neither of us wants to lose.

I can hear the sounds of my body. I can hear how wet I am. And Emory's unique scent seems to wrap all around me, that vanilla and caramel richness that I want to rub all over my skin. And even though he thinks he's so different from when we were little, I'm pretty damned sure he smells the way he did when we were young.

I want to tell him, but the words catch in my throat.

He takes me harder and harder, and I use my leverage against the shelf to meet each of his thrusts with my own. He makes a strangled sound and goes wild. I feel the moment his inner beast rises to the surface because that big dick of his gets bigger. My body stretches around him, and he locks into me, unable to leave until we're both done.

And god damn it, I love the way berserkers fuck. But with Emory? It's even better.

My eyes roll back in my head. I'm barely clinging onto him as he pounds into me harder and harder, his strength humming all around me. Suddenly, my inner muscles squeeze him, and my nerves scream, and then I'm orgasming.

Emory comes as I orgasm, his hot seed spilling into me as he shouts in pleasure.

For several long minutes, we keep going. A berserker moment of frenzy. A moment that can only happen between two of our kind. His cock spills his seed twice. More orgasms roll through me, over and over again, until every muscle in my body is little more than jello.

And then he crumbles to his knees, taking me with him.

He stays that way for a long time, capturing me between the books and his huge body.

At last, he starts to speak, his voice low and confused. "Kiera...we shouldn't...we shouldn't have..."

I bite his ear, still trying to catch my breath. "I think you meant...we should have done this sooner."

He looks at me, and his eyes gentle.

I stiffen. Something in his gaze is overwhelming. Like he's about to say something neither of us can take back. And as much as I want to hear it, I'm not sure I'm ready. But I'm also not sure I can stop him.

Behind us, someone clears her throat.

We both jerk toward the sound.

A woman stands at the end of the shelves, her arms crossed over her chest. She's petite, probably shorter than me, and that's saying something. Her hair is long and dark, silky smooth as it flows over her shoulders, and her expression is harsh.

"Why are two students fucking in the ancient magic section of the library? Don't you know fucking is for the psychology section? And why the hell is their blood on my floor?"

"Uh…" I have no idea what to tell her.

She lifts a brow and glances at the berserker brand on my arm. "I'm guessing you're Kiera, the female berserker?"

I nod.

"Get dressed and meet me in my office upstairs. Now!" Spinning on her heels, she marches away.

Emory draws slowly back from me, and we dress quickly. When we're done, I swear Emory plans to just walk away. And for some reason, that pisses me off.

"Were you following me before?"

He stops.

"You were. Why?"

"I just wanted to make sure you were safe."

"I'd be safer with you at my side, not hiding in the shadows behind me."

Emory slowly looks back at me, and a coolness has come over his face. "That's all I can give you. Now, come on, I'll show you her office."

He doesn't look back to see if I follow. He just walks away.

The tiny office is just a desk with a computer on it, a phone, and bookshelves squeezed in around us. When we enter, the librarian gives Emory a dirty look, but then directs her attention to me.

"You may call your family."

I stiffen. "I thought phone calls weren't allowed?"

She raises a brow. "You really want to question this?"

I shake my head, my pulse racing.

To my surprise, she leaves the room, closing the door behind us. Going around her desk, I sit in her seat and draw the phone closer. Staring at the handle, I don't know why I hesitate. I guess part of me fears that the second I hear my parent's voices, I might just lose it.

Still, they deserve to know I'm safe.

They deserve more than that.

"Careful," Emory says. "Maxen will have tried to get to your family. You might not like what you hear from them."

My eyes narrow. "You might have forgotten, Emory, but no one can break a Winter Berserker."

He looks like he might argue, but I start to dial.

The phone rings. Once. Twice. Three times. And with each ring, my heart beats faster. *What if they don't pick up? What if--?*

"Hello?" Mother's voice comes over the line, and I swear it's the sweetest sound I've ever heard.

"Mom?"

"Kiera." There's shock in her voice.

"I'm here."

I hear her shouting for my father and brothers, then, "You don't know how worried we've been. You don't know how scared we were when we heard—"

"Kiera!" Suddenly, my father and brothers are talking at once, launching questions at me, telling me how much they've missed me. I press my knuckles to my mouth and try to quiet my sobs as tears run down my face.

Emory shifts closer, but he doesn't touch me.

"Quiet! Quiet, everyone!" my mom says. "Let her talk."

And then they're silent.

I rub the tears from my face and take a deep breath, not wanting my family to know just how hard it's been to be away from them. "The vampires killed Lucy, and I went berserk. I didn't mean to. I didn't know I could. And then Emory—"

"Emory? Emory?" I hear my oldest brother ask, in shock.

I look at the big berserker, but his face gives nothing away. "Yeah, he was there. He tried to get me out of the club before they could get me, but they caught us both. And then we were at the reform school, and now Maxen is sending his thugs to try to get to me."

My words suddenly stop. *What else should I say?*

"Listen." This time it's my father's voice. "Maxen is dangerous. More dangerous than you can ever imagine. He's already…called us. But don't worry about us, there's nothing that bastard can do to us. But you have to stay safe. You can't marry him."

"I know, I'm trying."

"I want to talk to Emory. Is he there?"

I'm surprised. "Yeah, he is…"

"Put him on the phone."

I slowly hand the phone to Emory. Then I hold my breath.

What does this mean? Why did the librarian let us call? Did Maxen threaten my family? And why would my father want to talk to Emory?

But I don't have any of the answers. All I can do is watch Emory, ears straining, and wait.

Chapter Twenty-Four

EMORY

I hold the phone to my ear and feel my heart thudding against my ribcage. Kiera's dad had always been the father I never had. When my mother's boyfriend ignored me, when he seemed to see me more as an obligation than a child, Emmett Frost had taken me under his wing. He'd been the one to teach me how to fight, how to treat women, and how to be an honorable berserker.

He'd be disappointed to discover the man I'd become.

"Emory?"

His deep voice, filled with authority, awakens old memories inside of me, and I have to force myself to remain calm. "Yes, Lord Frost?"

"It's really you?"

"It is."

Silence swallows us both for a moment before he speaks. "I'm sorry about what happened to you. If I had known what exiling Jimmy would lead to, if I had known your mom didn't want the responsibility of you anymore, I would've taken you in as my own."

A shudder wracks my body. Fate was a cruel mistress. One single decision led me to a life of pain and suffering and loneliness. But in front of me I could see it all, the same choice made differently that could've meant a life of happiness, of kindness, of love.

"You couldn't have known," I say, but even I can hear the hurt in my voice.

"I knew who your father was," he admits softly, "but I never thought your mother would give you to him. She came to me seeking sanctuary. She knew what was in store for both of you if she remained at the House of Berserkers."

"And yet she dropped me off and left."

There's a pause. "Emory…you know there's no way your mother made it off your father's lands, right?"

I'm panting, my head spinning. "What?"

"Going there…she had no chance."

I rub my forehead, trying to calm my emotions. All these years, I'd hated my mom so much for what she'd done to me. I'd hated her for taking me away from my family with the Winter Berserkers and delivering me into hell. *But she was dead? I'd been hating a dead woman.*

"I'm so sorry."

I force the words past my lips. "It doesn't matter. It was a long time ago."

There's another long pause before he continues, "Can my daughter hear us?"

I glance up and take a step or two back from Kiera, as far as the cord can reach. "Not if we're quiet."

He speaks again, his voice lower. "Maxen is worse than his father, even though I thought such a thing was impossible. I can't risk Kiera being taken by him. So, I reached out to the other lords. I thought if one of them would agree to marry her, she'd be safe."

My heart aches. "That's smart."

"Emory, none of them would do it. None of them would risk Maxen's wrath."

My hands clench into fists. I hadn't wanted to see Kiera with another man, but I also knew it was the smartest thing I could do. But now…now that option was gone.

"So we have to keep her away from them."

"Or," and his voice drops even lower, "you marry her, and we have you take Maxen's throne."

"What? No!"

Kiera's gaze narrows, and I turn my back to her, heart racing. I did not want to rule over anyone. How could I when every single person I tried to protect had died at Maxen's hands? How could I lead when I couldn't keep anyone safe, not even myself?

I did *not* want to be responsible for Kiera's life. I would fail her. It was inevitable.

"You need to find someone else."

"There is no one else. Technically, you were born before your brother. Many believe that the gods meant for you to lead the House of Berserkers. If you marry my daughter, it will reinforce that belief. The other lords will not go against the gods; they'll remove Maxen and we'll all be safe. It's the only way."

I shake my head. "You don't understand. You don't know who I am now. I'm not the man you think I am. I'm not—"

"Emory, you have a good heart. You know right from wrong. Life led us down different paths, but I always thought you'd be one of the men my daughter would marry. Why not now? When it could protect her?"

"I'm not…strong enough. Please don't ask this of me."

Lord Frost grows quiet. "Can you think of any other way to ensure she'll never fall into his hands?"

I open my mouth, but the truth was that I couldn't.

"Please, Emory, think about it."

"Okay," I say, but I feel like I'm tumbling down a hole.

"I need to ask something more of you."

More than marrying his daughter? "Yes?"

"Keep her safe."

I stiffen. "Of course."

"No," and the word comes out a growl. "Give me your word that you'll keep her safe."

My word. My word means nothing. So why don't I want to give it?

"Emory."

"You have my word. I'll keep her safe." The words are some of the heaviest of my life.

"Thank you." He exhales slowly. "Can we speak to our daughter?"

I hand the phone back to Kiera and crumble into a chair. *Me as Kiera's husband? Me as a leader of a house?* It wasn't possible. I wasn't a leader. I was too broken.

And then I think of going against my brother and shiver. If Lord Frost knew just how twisted Maxen was, he would never go against him. Lord Frost was accustomed to running things, to being a beacon of hope to his people. He had never lived in the shadow of a monster.

He didn't understand that there was no winning against evil.

I don't know how much time passes when Kiera says goodbye, wipes the tears from her face, and stands. It takes me a long moment to remind myself not to touch her, not to comfort her. And I hate that those instincts are there. I hate that it feels like whatever power had connected us all these years was solidified into something unbreakable the moment we touched.

I loved her. There was no denying it.

And yet, it didn't matter. None of it mattered except keeping her safe and coming up with a plan to do so that didn't involve us marrying.

My legs still shake when I rise from the chair, not knowing what to say. Not knowing what to do. We'd just had sex. Somehow she'd been allowed to call her family. And her dad had asked me to marry her.

What the hell was I supposed to do?

Her gaze meets mine, and I look away. "What did my father ask you to do?"

She's too damned smart. "I don't want to talk about it."

"Emory—"

"We have class." I know I'm running away from her and the whole situation when I open the door and head out, but I must be a coward, because I keep going.

Not far outside the door, the librarian is putting books on shelves. She frowns at us when we emerge. As we move to walk past her, her stern voice stops us. "Whoever your family is, they're powerful. Students never get phone calls."

I don't tell her that I doubt that Kiera's parents were able to request a phone call, because then I'd have to explain. I'd have to explain to both of them that Maxen probably arranged it. And that her parents were probably threatened. Maxen no doubt hoped they'd tell her, and it'd compel her to marry him.

How could he have known just how stubborn Lord Frost was?

We leave the library, and Kiera matches my stride with her much smaller legs. I can tell she has a thousand things she wants to say, but I hope she doesn't. I have no idea what to tell her about having sex with her. It was incredible. It was everything I'd always wanted and more. And yet, it was wrong of me.

Kiera deserved better.

It wasn't a mistake I'd soon make again.

As we start to pass the training yard, I try to ignore the men wrestling together on the dirt, but my instincts having been screaming since Maxen's men approached me. Kiera might be fearless, but that's because she didn't know what my brother was capable of. I would have to be more careful for the both of us.

When we pass the men, one of them calls my name.

I startle and turn slowly around. Jasper is among the men. Guilt weighs heavy on me as I stare at the man who has spent most of his life here. I don't know how he managed to survive the cullings each year and neither die nor be released, but I was sure my brother had something to do with it.

My gaze moves over the other three men. A massive man who had to be a bear shifter, a male mermaid with dark hair, and a phoenix with his sad, broken wings behind him.

Kiera stares at them beside me, frowning.

Jasper approaches. "You've been missing a lot of classes. They're talking about stringing you up in the courtyard." His expression gives nothing away. "But they'll probably just whip your flesh raw."

"Thanks for the heads up," I say, and for some reason my hand twitches to reach for my sword.

"Not that you'll live that long."

I whirl around and spot the four warlocks who have appeared not far behind Kiera and I. In an instant, I've drawn my sword and Kiera holds her axes. Both of us ready ourselves for a fight, but my eyes snap from the four men behind us to the four men before us.

That's what was wrong. That's why my instinct had warned me about: these men. A phoenix, a mermaid, a shifter, and a berserker would never be caught dead together. But if given the right incentive by my brother, they'd do anything.

"Give her to us," Jasper says, sounding tired, "and no one needs to die."

"You're still working for him? After everything he did? After he left you here?" I ask, the outrage bleeding into my words.

He holds my gaze. "He offered me the one thing worth working with him again: my freedom. Now, Emory, don't do this. Just give her to us."

I rotate my sword, my gaze snapping between all of them. "Find Drake and Adam," I tell Kiera softly. "I'll try to hold them back."

"What? No!"

"Do it!" *Why the hell couldn't she just listen to me?*

And then it's too late.

Magic sparkles across my skin from the warlocks, and I feel the sparks of fire burning into my flesh. But if they thought pain could distract me, they were wrong. Pain I understood. My grip on my sword never wavers.

Behind me, Jasper starts to change, and my heart goes in my throat. If I completely gave into that side of me, I wouldn't be able to make the right decisions. I'd kill and kill, but I might lose Kiera without even realizing.

So I reach for that side of myself, but I don't let myself go too far. Just until the burns stop hurting. Just until the magic that slices through my chest is little more than a sting. When Jasper attacks, I block his path from Kiera and hold my blade out in front of me. The mermaid is just behind him, ready to do his own kind of damage. But with care, I shove Jasper as he approaches, sending the muscular berserker crashing to the earth, and then slice the head off the mermaid in one movement.

Jasper roars on the ground and struggles to rise.

The bear shift manages to get around me, but Kiera uses those axes of hers, slicing the beast. One of his paws manages to tear deep scratches into her arm, and then I see red. I leap onto the beast, and we tumble together, snarls rising between us. His paws swipe my flesh, but the pain is nothing. My sword presses past those powerful claws of his, and then I tear open his throat, bathing myself in blood.

I leap to my feet and see Kiera's axes clashing with the phoenix's sword. I race for them, but a massive body comes crashing into me from the side. Jasper. His hands close around my throat, squeezing, and my hands grasp his throat, crushing the muscles. Together we watch the life draining from each other's eyes, seeing who will die first, and then the warlocks are standing over me.

One minute my vision is darkening around the edges, but I know Jasper's will is weaker than mine, and the next a cloud of red cloaks me, and the world goes black.

I try to shout for Kiera, to beg her to run again before the darkness takes me under, but I'm not sure I manage to say anything before I'm gone.

Chapter Twenty-Five

ADAM

*D*rake and I are walking back from the dining hall, like friends, like *real* friends. Even though we don't hold hands. I'm happy, glad to have shared a meal with him, even though we both missed Kiera and Emory at the table.

It gave us time to get to know each other. He didn't talk much, but I talked enough for both of us. And I knew he liked me too, because he only growled a little when I ate off his plate.

Which was better than last week when he smacked the fork from my hand.

I'm feeling good. My heart is soaring. I have two friends. I have Kiera. I have everything.

Even if we never escape, I could be happy here with them.

But as I'm about to tell Drake my feelings, something he keeps reminding me I don't need to do, I spot a bloody figure on the ground near the training yard. Without thought, I race forward and turn the man onto his back, only to find Emory. My hands reach for his face, and I feel the dark magic that holds him in a mind full of pain. A dark world of suffering.

Somebody hurt him? But who? Panic awakens, making my heart hurt, but I force myself to push the feeling down. I've seen the work of warlocks before. I know how to help him.

Pushing my powers out, I break through the darkness. I absorb the powers, like a vacuum sucking up smoke, and then cleanse the cloud of its danger until there's nothing left, and release the nothingness back into the world. At last, Emory takes a ragged breath, and my gaze runs over the many, many wounds that litter his body.

Can I heal them? I shiver. My creators taught me how to do many, many things. But few of them were natural things. My body didn't like the powers, and my body punished me when I used them.

So, I don't. I don't try. This is not the time to be useless.

"What happened?" Drake snarls behind me. "Where's Kiera?"

Kiera? No. Kiera has to be safe. She *has* to be.

Emory stares at us, until his eyes focus on Drake, and then he says, his voice weak, "They took her."

My heart seems to turn to ice. *Kiera. They took Kiera?*

"Where? Who?" Drake shouts.

"To the gate. If they've already opened it, if his men have already taken her…"

"No!" Drake roars, the sound of anguish the same terrible feeling that radiates through my heart.

He hauls Emory to his feet like he's a rag doll, and then he's running to the gate, dragging Emory until the berserker finds his footing, and then they're both running. I rise to my feet and follow them, overtaking them with ease, but I'm not like them. I'm not ready for battle.

But even more so, I can't imagine losing Kiera now.

As the wind whips around me, I remember the lab I

was created within. I remember the many different creatures that they merged with my own genetics. From the first time Kiera and I had touched, I'd felt something powerful between us. I'd thought it might be the shifter part of me, the part of me that chose a mate and couldn't live without them.

But then I remembered a show I'd seen long ago. I remembered the penguins. Their connection wasn't magic like it was with the shifters. It was something else. Something more natural. When they chose a partner, it was for eternity. Without them, there was no one else.

And when they died, those without mates would sometimes stand together. They would watch the sun rise and fall, and, I swore, morn their lost partners.

I think Kiera is my penguin.

I love her when we touch. I love her when I'm inside her. But I also love the way she laughs, the way she defends me, and even the way she seems to understand my connection with Princess, without me even needing to explain it.

Kiera *is* my penguin. And I won't watch the sunrise with Drake and Emory and think of her. Not when I can still save her.

No matter what I have to do.

We're nearly to the gate when an alarm sounds. Never in my time at the reform school have I heard an alarm sound, and it makes me think the worst. That it's too late.

But I only run faster. Harder.

It takes no time at all to race through the massive trial grounds, but already I can see the smoke from the enormous school gates. A sound booms through the air, and the ground shakes beneath our feet. I watch in shock as the huge doors are battered in, flames crumbling along with the gate.

In front of us, Kiera stands in the middle of a group of

men. Her hands are bound. She bleeds from several places, but still she fights them as they start to haul her closer to the door.

Another earthquake seems to shake the ground, but this time behind us. I chance a glance back, and my jaw drops. A massive black dragon rises, bigger than the buildings, bigger than the trial space itself. He tosses back his head and lets out a roar that ends in fire that scorches the sky.

Suddenly, he steps over me, and I stop running, my heart racing.

He leans over the men that hold Kiera and in one bite eats two of them. Another man screams and leaps back from her. A red-haired man looks between the dragon and the gates.

Emory is there in an instant, slicing his throat. The red-haired man crumbles to his knees, and I attack the remaining man, a sick feeling in my belly when he falls, unmoving, to the ground.

As I step over the body, I see that Emory is cutting Kiera free. She grabs her axes from the crumbled body on the ground and resheaths them, kicking the body.

And then I'm there, pulling her into my arms, my heart soaring.

Kiera was safe. We'd gotten to her in time.

Climb onto my back. The voice that rolls through my mind is different from Princess's. It's louder, angrier, a twisted version of Drake's voice.

We look at him as he lowers himself to the ground. Kiera doesn't hesitate; she climbs up his body and onto his back, and so I follow, sitting behind her. Emory pauses, resheaths his sword, and then joins us.

"I thought you couldn't fly," I say.

I've been practicing.

"So you can?"

We'll see.

He begins to flap his massive wings. I stare at them, seeing the scars that connect the delicate tissue. Wondering if, in all his practicing, he's had a successful flight.

Ahead of us, I hear the sounds of magic exploding. I look beyond the flaming, broken gates, and spot a group of men standing around a car. In the center of them, I know, is Maxen. There's something about him that reminds me of an evil version of his brother. Something I can't quite put my finger on.

Behind me, I feel a tremble wrack Emory's body, and I wish I could say or do something to take away his fear. But then we launch into the air. Drake's big wings flap and flap, but the launch is anything but elegant. He struggles, his flight uneven. But we manage to pass the school gate, skimming just above the trees.

I sense more magic exploding behind us, but Drake continues forward. With every second I think we're going to crash, that we're going to drop into the trees below, but Drake keeps us safe.

"You can fly," I hear Kiera whisper from in front of me. "You can really fly."

Drake says nothing, but I can feel his pleasure.

Never before have I dreamed of flying. But now that I am, I find that I like it. I like the fresh air. I like the feeling of nothingness and everything around us.

"I like flying," I say.

"It's like a dream," Emory whispers.

And then I have that terrible feeling again. The feeling of dark magic. I turn around and spot a massive ball of black flames rushing toward us.

"Drake, watch out!" I scream.

As Drake turns, twisting in the air to avoid it, we all

slide and nearly fall from his back. But the ball of darkness slips past us. Drake begins to right himself, and we have one moment of relief before the black ball turns back around.

"Drake!"

You'll fall, he says, and even though he tries to twist the other way again, I can tell he's trying to keep us safe.

Which is his downfall.

The black magic strikes one of his wings, and he screams, a horrible sound worse than the final sounds of a dying phoenix. He plummets to the ground, and I take a deep breath and try to do something I haven't done since the scientists made me. Because this time, we'll die if I don't.

I push out the force around me, trying to protect us all from the impact. The blue glowing ball expands around me, and out far enough that I pray it will protect Emory and Kiera too. But when I try to push it out to protect Drake, we hit the trees.

His massive body crashes, smashing into tree after tree before he slowly comes to a stop. Unmoving.

"Drake!" Kiera screams, and the ball of blue around us fades.

She scrambles off of his back and comes to his face. Her hands touch his scales gently, but his eyes don't open.

I try to go after her, but I simply collapse. The shield… I never liked it. Afterwards I was as weak as a babe. And being weak with the scientists was dangerous.

"What's wrong with you?" Emory asks, sounding breathless.

"The magic…"

He grunts, and suddenly he lifts me onto his shoulders before sliding down Drake. I can feel with Emory something that I've never felt before. The way his body trembles. The way the wounds on his body aren't even attempting to close.

He's weak. Weaker than he's letting on.

"Drake," Kiera whispers, and tears slide down her face.

"We need to keep going," Emory says.

Kiera looks back at him. "We can't leave him like this."

"He needs to shift. If he can go back to his human form, we can take him with us."

I'll be too weak, rumbles in my mind.

"We have to do this. Before they reach us."

"Put me down," I tell Emory.

He does so, but my legs collapse beneath me. It takes me a few tries to stand. But when I do, I finally see the group of us. We look like hell. But Emory was right, we needed to run before the bad men found us.

But could Drake shift in this bad of shape? Anyone would tell him not to. That his shifter body would heal faster, and that he'd be stronger should he be attacked. But we couldn't exactly drag a dragon with us.

So what will he do?

I'm still not sure when his body begins to shimmer and shrink. Within seconds, the massive dragon has been replaced by Drake. Only, it's not Drake.

I gasp and go to him, kneeling beside him. There's nothing left of his skin. He bleeds everywhere, and one of his arms and his leg are definitely broken. And given the harsh way he breathes, his lungs can't be much better.

"We have to go," Emory says, and he limps forward and gently lifts Drake into his arms.

The dragon shifter screams, and the sound makes tears prickle my eyes. That kind of pain…most people would never know that kind of pain, but I do.

When this is over, I wouldn't eat off his plate. I

wouldn't hold his hand. And I wouldn't tell him my feelings so much.

I *would* pat him on the back. *A lot.*

Kiera rubs away the tears that race down her face. "Which…way?"

Emory doesn't answer, he just picks a direction.

Kiera presses a hand over her injured arm, covered in deep gashes, and I stagger along behind. Emory doesn't have to tell us that we need to get as far as fast as we can from the dragon-sized imprint in the forest.

But still, our going is slow.

Hours pass. We're all breathing hard. Emory's eyes keep closing as he stumbles forward, and Drake is in and out of consciousness.

And yet, there's been no signs of Maxen. *So maybe we'll get free? Maybe Kiera will be safe.*

Hope blossoms in my heart.

And then we'll be free. From him. From the reform school. And it'll just be us.

Who says mutants don't get happy endings?

Chapter Twenty-Six

KIERA

The sun is setting when we reach a hill. We all know we need to slow soon, that we can't just keep trudging forward, and that we need to find a place to hide until morning. But so far, fear has kept us going.

The thing is, we need to rest. Not just because we can't go on much longer, but because we need to heal. And we heal much faster when we sleep.

Which Drake needs, desperately.

My heart twists. I have never seen injuries as bad as his. I knew shifters could heal from almost anything, but I didn't have a clue how his body could fix what had happened to him.

And then there was Emory. Most of his wounds had stopped bleeding, but he was a mess of cuts, bruises, and injuries. Most berserkers would have to sleep for hours after enduring something like that.

But not Emory. He just trudged on.

Something in my chest warms. I hadn't been happy about how cold he'd been after we'd slept together, but I had to accept that even if Emory wasn't the same boy I knew, he was still a good man. A man I was lucky to have at my side.

My gaze moves to Adam, and then back ahead of me as I try not to stumble. Adam had used a power I'd never seen before. And in doing so, he'd saved us. I didn't know what he'd done, but when this was all over, I was going to ask him about it.

"After…this hill…" Emory says, gasping in breaths. "We find…a place…to stop."

We all move a little faster after that, but when we crest the hill Emory freezes. Adam and I come up behind him and look down in shock. A road stretches out before us, and sitting in the middle of the road are three black cars, and the same men who shot us down.

One man smiles.

Maxen. The asshole himself. A chill rolls down my spine, and I glance at the half a dozen men that stand around him. I knew some of them were mages. Powerful mages. And some were vamps and berserkers.

I feel sick as sweat rolls down my back. We can't outrun them. I guess we'd have to fight them.

I'd have to fight them.

"It took you all long enough."

"No," Adam says, and the word sounds tortured, echoing the feeling inside of me.

"It was a true test of your will, but the spell my warlocks weaved was always going to lead you here. To me."

"You bastard!" I scream, drawing my axes from my back and standing in front of my men.

This time, I would face him head on. This time, I would fight with my dying breath.

His gaze runs over me, far too slowly. "Kiera Frost of the Winter Berserkers, I'm glad to meet you. I am King

Maxen Wolff of the House of Berserkers, and your future husband."

"I'll die before I marry you," I growl.

He grins. "Too bad I'm not giving you the choice."

"The bond can't be forced," I tell him, my heart racing.

"Oh." His smile widens. "Who said anything about forcing you?"

I take another step forward. "I challenge you, Maxen, false king of the berserkers. One warrior to another. Winner takes all."

He laughs. "That challenge is for males, Kiera."

"Are you afraid?"

"No, my sweet, I simply don't wish to hurt you." His gaze slides to Emory. "Is that the dragon and the mutant I've heard so much about? We'll bring them with us, Emory. One never knows when a life might have a use."

My hands tighten on my axes. "If you think for one second—"

Emory steps out in front of me, still carrying Drake, and heads down the hill.

"Emory, no!"

For a moment, I'm too shocked to react. In another time or another place, I might have dug my axe into Emory's back and saved Drake. But something in me can't process it, can't believe it, when Emory walks away from us and joins Maxen's side.

Adam is beside me in an instant, and we both stare in shock as Emory dumps Drake's body in the trunk of one of the cars.

"Emory. We're friends," Adam says, and his voice is so damned innocent.

Emory comes to stand beside his brother, and Maxen sets his hand on the berserker's shoulder. "I'm afraid that's what Emory had to pretend to be to bring me my bride. But he isn't capable of friendship. He isn't capable of anything. Now, are you coming with me willingly, or should we separate your dragon from his head?"

"He would want you to run," Adam whispers in my ear.

He would. But I can't. "Go, Adam. Run. They won't go after you if they have me."

I don't turn to see if he obeys me. I resheath my axes and come toward Maxen, my stomach twisting. Hating him more with every step I take.

When I stop in front of Maxen, my gaze slides to Emory. His expression is blank. He simply stares ahead without even the hint of guilt.

And something breaks inside of me at that moment. I realize that even when he walked away, I hoped this was a trick. That he had some kind of plan up his sleeve to save us all.

But now, I see. And I hate myself for it. Emory never pretended to be anything he wasn't. He never pretended this was anything but trying to make us even.

I should have listened.

"I can't believe I trusted you," I say, and hate how heartbroken I sound.

Maxen sets his hands on my shoulder. "You aren't the first to be fooled by him."

I jerk back from the man, and anger flashes in his eyes.

"Careful, Kiera. We wouldn't want to get off on the wrong foot."

"Fuck you!"

He smirks. "Get in the car. We'll clear this up at home."

Suddenly, two of his men step forward, and Adam is dragged forward. I whirl around and stare at him in shock.

"I said to—"

"I could never just leave," he whispers softly.

Maxen's eyes seem to drink in Adam. "A talking, walking mutant… Oh, you are going to be fun. Put him in the trunk with the meat bag."

I'm shoved into the back of the car, even as I struggle to see Adam. In his face I see fear, but not surrender, and steel uncurls in my spine.

Maxen might have won this round.

But we would win the next.

And when we were done? I swore I would watch as the life drained from his eyes.

We drive away from the Wicked Reform School, me squeezed between Emory and Maxen.

I could feel Maxen's eyes on me, and so I smile.

Let him see. Let him see that Kiera Frost of the Winter Berserkers would not be defeated. No matter what he did to me, I would never be like Emory.

I had the heart of a berserker. And berserkers never gave up.

Did you enjoy Untamed? Enjoy the next book in the Wicked Reform School, Narcotize! And if you want to preorder the next book that follows Kiera and her men, preorder your copy of Unknown.

Books in the Wicked Reform School

Untamed: House of Berserkers by Lacey Carter Andersen
Narcotized: House of Mermaids by TB Mann
Avarice: House of Mustelid by Emma Cole
Reborn: House of Phoenix by Lia Davis
Bloodlust: House of Vampires by Tabitha Barret
Revenge: House of Nephilim by May Dawson
Rebel: House of Fae by Rosemary A Johns

Want more from Lacey Carter Andersen?

Sign up for exclusive first looks at my hot new releases, exclusives, and contests from Lacey Carter Andersen!

Want to be part of the writing process? Maybe even get a taste of my sense of humor? Teasers for my new releases? And more? Join Lacey's Realm on Facebook!

Also By Lacey Carter Andersen

Paranormal Prison

Wraith Captive

Marked Immortals

Wicked Reform School/House of Berserkers

Untamed: House of Berserkers

Unknown: House of Berserkers

Monsters and Gargoyles

Medusa's Destiny *audiobook*

Keto's Tale

Celaeno's Fate

Cerberus Unleashed

Lamia's Blood

Shade's Secret

Shorts: Their Own Sanctuary

Shorts: Their Miracle Pregnancy

Dark Supernaturals

Wraith Captive

Marked Immortals

Mates of the Realms

Renegade Hunter *audiobook*

Cursed Hunter

Betrayed Hunter

Rebel Lover

Rebel Lies

Rebel Loss

Rogue Demon

Box Set I: Demon Hunter

Box Set II: Rebel Angel

The Firehouse Feline

Feline the Heat

Feline the Flames

Feline the Burn

God Fire Reform School

Magic for Dummies

Myths for Half-Wits

Legends Unleashed

Don't Say My Name

Don't Cross My Path

Alternative Futures

Nightmare Hunter *audiobook*

Deadly Dreams *audiobook*

Mortal Flames

Twisted Prophecies

Box Set: Alien Mischief

An Icelius Reverse Harem

Her Alien Lovers

Her Alien Abductors

Her Alien Barbarians

Her Alien Mates

Collection: Her Alien Romance

Steamy Tales of Warriors and Rebels

Gladiators

The Dragon Shifters' Last Hope

Stolen by Her Harem

Claimed by Her Harem

Treasured by Her Harem

Collection: Magic in her Harem

Harem of the Shifter Queen

Sultry Fire

Sinful Ice

Saucy Mist

Collection:Power in her Kiss

Standalones

Goddess of Love (Blood Moon Rising Shared World)

Worthy (A Villainously Romantic Retelling)

Beauty with a Bite

Shifters and Alphas

Collections

Monsters, Gods, Witches, Oh My!

Wings, Horns, and Shifters

About the Author

Lacey Carter Andersen loves reading, writing, and drinking excessive amounts of coffee. She spends her days taking care of her husband, three kids, and three cats. But at night, everything changes! Her imagination runs wild with strong-willed characters, unique worlds, and exciting plots that she enthusiastically puts into stories.

Lacey has dozens of tales: science fiction romances, paranormal romances, short romances, reverse harem romances, and more. So, please feel free to dive into any of her worlds; she loves to have the company!

And you're welcome to reach out to her; she really enjoys hearing from her readers.

You can find her at:

Email: laceycarterandersen@gmail.com

Mailing List: https://www.subscribepage.com/laceycarterandersen

Website: www.laceycarterandersen.wordpress.com/

Facebook Page: www.facebook.com/Lacey-Carter-Andersen-1940678949483316/